GW00419731

April 2023

To
AOIBHEANN

WITH Best Wishes

NIGHT MUSIC

Fergus Cronin

Doire Press

First published in 2023

Doire Press
Aille, Inverin
Co. Galway
www.doirepress.com

Layout: Lisa Frank
Cover design: Tríona Walsh
Cover image: *Toward the Cross* by Dominic Turner
www.dominicturner.ie
Author photo: Emily Quinn
www.emilyquinn.com

Printed by Clódóirí CL
Casla, Co. na Gaillimhe

ISBN 978-1-907682-94-0

We gratefully acknowledge the support and assistance of The Arts Council / An Chomhairle Ealaíon.

CONTENTS

For Maur

ALL THAT JAZZ

It may have been in Ronnie Scott's — Jack Bruce storming his way through a driving *Politician* — or it could have been in the Bricklayer's Arms at a Curved Air gig, where only the naked drummer was more drenched than myself, but on one of those sweaty nights it had first occurred to me to try to get in touch with Sean, my uncle, the navvy. He surely had a London to offer that didn't just throb so beautifully, and damage my head so much.

*

The hallway with the pay phone was the coldest place in that cold house in North London where I lived in 1971. It was where the calls home were made or, the odd time, taken. A marmalade cat skulked in the gloom there. I had a number for Sean written on a fag packet from the day, a few years earlier, we'd spent at the Fairy-house Races. Yeah, *that* day. Maybe it would work. It did. After the shrill landlady came the familiar Mayo-London accent, all hesitant and tuneful.

'Hello. Who's this?'

'It's Ger, Sean.'

'Who?'

'Ger. Your nephew. Gerry.'

There was a pretty long silence. It was late evening so he would've been drinking at some stage. This could go anywhere. Nothing, and then finally, after what might have been a sigh or simple exasperation, his voice came again in a lower register.

'Yes. I know.' A further long pause. 'Gerry, yes. Where are you now?'

*

As soon as I hit ground level at Tooting Bec, I sensed something different — more normal and somehow reas-suring. I headed up towards the Common and the Rose and Crown. Sean had said the name of the bar in that shy sing-songy mumble. He rarely made complete sen-tences, but I knew how to interpret his meaning from the fragments. As we sat up to the bar, it was clear that he didn't make much of my get-up.

'Do you need shoes?' He'd boiled it down to that one, but I knew he was asking a world of questions in that.

'I've a bit of work in a hotel. Inside work.' That would explain the shabby desert boots, but even as I said it I was already involved in his reaction, so I went on. 'It's okay for now but I'd like to get something, you know, better.'

'What, like teaching? A teacher?' He was looking over at the fruit machine as he savoured the word.

'Your mammy said you... qualified.' He liked the taste of that one too. Had his whole menu of words to chew on. I had to accept he might be pressing a number of different buttons. He might be trying to suggest something useful or he could well be putting me down. Sean was intelligent. I watched him look at the two pints settling on the counter. He reached for one with his shovel hand and took a big slug. I watched his dreamy blood-shot stare, looking out, away. Slow and easy with everything, worming his way back along the memory lines.

'I did yeah, a few years ago. You were talking to her since? My father?' I knew the answer of course. He turned fairly sharply to look straight at me, right into my eyes, and lowered his glass — mostly empty by now. He suspended the glass on its way down to the counter and turned his focus, for a long moment, to the John Lennon badge on my lapel. It said 'Give Peace a Chance'. The glooky eyes could have been on a fish tray in Billingsgate. When he'd finished saying whatever he was saying, without ever opening his mouth — which was now a sort of scowl — he finally put the glass down, his eyes, burning and pained, following it all the way. After a while he spoke quietly, not looking at me.

'How is your mammy?'

It was amazing how fast the alcohol grabbed his levers. Took him not necessarily to drunkenness but to some other ethereal place where he operated best. More comfortably. The grimace and lip-licking after the swallow. The shrinking away of the body like everything physical needed to be hidden. Leaving only the thinking — held together behind those urgent eyes — and the distortions of the mouth. He wore a stained, light brown gaberdine coat and a grimy shirt collar fell away from the weathered grizzle that was his neck. His handsome leather shoes were planted on the brass footrail in an easy restful manner — work-boots, like the blistering tools, were set aside after the day. He minded his feet like they were the only part of him that mattered. The greying hair was trim and was matched by the bristles on the heightening colour of his creviced face. How in the name of Jesus did I find any comfort in this? But I did. I did, because it meant something.

'Mam's fine. I spoke to her last week.' I waited. 'Dad hasn't been well. You know about the MS.'

'Are there any doctors in that country? Do they know their trade at all? Here you get the NHS.' He sucked on those letters. 'The National Health Service. Nye Bevan. You ever hear of Nye Bevan? Of course you did. You're the clever one. Oh yes! The National Health Service. The Road to Wigan Pier.'

Was that last bit meant as a gibe, an irony — my father now the comfortable middle-class man? Or was he saying something about his own disillusionment? He hadn't spoken to my father in twenty years, not since I was a small child. He used to come and stay with us then, on his way back to see his mother in the west. Ballybrohan, near Knock. Their father, an old RIC constable, had lived peacefully until he died in the forties. My grandmother (with her hat-pin) was gone less than ten years now but Sean still made that long trip by boat and train every year to see his sister who lived on, alone, in the small, terraced family house. In that damp grey place where small birds sang plaintive songs within earshot of the cold hammering and chiselling from a stonecutter's yard. He continued.

'MS. Your mammy's a good woman. Her people are from Wales. Railway people. Working people. Cardiff Arms Park. Big yellow daffodils.'

He phoned my mother every so often but would hang up if my father answered. They had no number for him, and he made me swear not to have them contact him when he wrote the number for me on the fag-packet that day. I'd been living at home studying for my final exams when, out of the blue, he'd called one evening and asked to speak with me. We met and went to the races, drank 'porter' — he liked words that sought to find me out — and helped to push cars from a mirey field of a car park. Then we did a crawl around his favourite Dublin bars and ended up at Harkin's, my bar, but he was barred as soon as he burst in the door all a-song, the county Meath mud caked on his new Oxfords and splashed over his swinging gaberdine. Stopped in his tracks so, he looked in despair at the crowd of long-haired students and turned on his heels and left. That was the last I'd seen of him until that night in Tooting.

*

That first night with him in London descended into a dim slur of alcohol. I woke up on a hard linoleum floor in a room with a rumpled bed and the smell of fried meat. I was in his digs and he was gone to a site. His shoes were placed neatly under a chair. There was a cooker in the corner. A couple of dry pots with some cold floury potatoes and half a turnip. A sooty pan displayed a burnt rasher and a limp pink sausage. On a table there were two greasy plates, a dozen or so empty stout bottles and a note with the word 'Sunday' and the name of another pub on the Common.

*

'How do yeh know Knocky?' The man with the dark-grained features spoke over the din, without looking at me, as he leaned in and left down an empty pint glass on the counter. I'd felt his taut body find the gap and force me to face him. He struck me as animal-like — the raven sheen of hair on the tanned muscular arms jutting from the rolled-up sleeves of the white shirt. They all wore white shirts at this end of the bar. Bri-Nylon dazzling in the early afternoon light. Knocky Gilvarry and his mates. Cleaned up for Easter Sunday.

'I'm related to him. Knocky? This place is mad.'

'Mad? There's nothing mad in here. Are you some

sort of a student or what?' He was staring at me now, at my long brown hair and pink cheesecloth shirt. His black eyes stormy.

'Tipp. Take it handy with the lad now. This is Gerry, my nephew.' Sean had nudged in. 'Tipp here is from—'

'Donohill. Plasterers. Dan Breen country. You've never heard of it I'd say.' The Tipperary man knew where he was from.

'I've heard of Dan Breen. He was a gunman?' I tried to sound wise.

'Careful what you say about gunmen here.' The whisper from the Tipp Raven was vehement.

A clatter of thoughts hit me. I looked around at the milling whiteness. There was one lean-looking character a little apart. He had a lily-emblem pinned to his shirt.

For some reason I felt glad that I'd decided not to wear any of my own badges.

'Don't mind that, Gerry. We're just working men here. Honest labour.' Sean had watched me take it all in.

'Labour my hole.' Tipp man was in like a shot at Sean.

'They're better than the other lot. Heath. A choir-boy.' Sean towered over the din.

'Haven't done much for the North.' The lily-man joined in — with a thin North of Ireland accent.

And so it went on. The darkness and the garbling and the jibing as this bunch of McAlpine's men went about their holy remembrances with an alcoholic fervour. The frothy, harrowed, celebrants vested in cut-off albs. I'd noticed that the far end of the bar, beyond the whirring, tinkling, bananas, oranges and lemons, was taken over completely by dark-skinned men. West-Indians.

'Nice blokes. But you wouldn't want to get in a scrap with them. Fight dirty. Blades.' Sean was in good form and home hadn't been mentioned. Then he was reciting the names of an Irish rugby team in my ear. He added my name. For some reason he did that.

'W.J. McBride... K.G. Goodall... R.A. Lamont... C.M.H Gibson... A.J.F O'Reilly... G.M.F Gilvarry. Twickenham. Yes.'

His own thing. That and his socialist heroes. The line on which he held his beliefs. I kind of got the irony in it all. The others had descended into litanies of Gaelic players, parishes, matches, scores. Now and again particular names or phrases could be heard among all the shouting.

'Boy Mick O'Connell boy.'

'Valentia Island.'

'Joe Fucking Corcoran Sean.'

'G'wan ya boy ya.'

'Some boy Willie Bryan boy.'

There was something close to a scream from a very drunk little man with a strong Dublin accent, who obviously lacked self-awareness.

'Charlie George. Gunners for the double.'

It disrupted the general hullabaloo; turned it into an embarrassed silence that lasted a good few seconds before the rumble of noise got back on its feet, a little uncertainly. Every one of those men managed to corner me on my own at some point, and hit me with questions about home. They would drop their guard as I gave them answers I thought they might like and then, for a moment or so, they would have a forlorn look that you might see on a beast lost on a country roadside.

The 'Caribbean' quarter was all pearly broad smiles and laughter. One of their number came over. He moved in a kind of happy shuffle.

'How are the Irish boys today? You men are so-oo sad. Give up a happy face. Ey mon?' He'd picked me out and held up a slap-hand. Tipp went to move in but Sean gripped his shoulder and held him back.

'No hassle man.' I slapped his hand high. It was the first time I'd used any of that jive language in Sean's company and I saw that his eyes clouded over and he seemed to sink a bit.

Later the place quietened down. The light outside the massive Victorian glazing had faded as a pink evening sky came on, the two of us side by side at the bar. The conversation inevitably turned to home. Sean wasn't drunk as such — he had massive capacity — but he wasn't sober either. I'd slowed down a bit and was hanging in. Sean turned to me, away from the two empty glasses on the counter. He'd gathered himself.

'You know I don't go with all that jazz.'

'What jazz do you mean?' I really hadn't a clue.

'You know... your... father.' He was neither soft nor hard on the word but I could see he was having difficulty with it. Jazz and my father? I didn't think so. Couldn't put that together.

'I mean he's done okay I suppose. For himself. Your mother. You. I just... really can't forget... Look I... what I'm saying is his life, the way he lives.'

'What about the way he lives? You mean he's not like you. He didn't choose to live in the ditch?'

'Hold your horses there. He left his own class.

Turned his back. All that dinner-dance carry-on and fancy carpets. And the golf. Those American magazines. *Golf this. Arnie that.* We were never like that. At home.' He held his hand up to the barman, flustered.

'What? You're not going to tell me by any chance that you were working-class people? That's a laugh. Your mother was from the big shop.'

I could see his pain through all the bluster and it was trying me. I'd wondered was there jealousy — sure there had to be — but I also remembered the family lore. Sean: the eldest, the brightest, working after school to bring in a few more shillings to help look after the younger ones; falling in with an older, dandy crowd— the doggies and the beer; paralysing him so he couldn't move beyond it all. Finally he'd packed up and left for the big world. There were rumours he'd been in the RAF, in Rhodesia, but he never said it to anyone in the family. What we did know is that he had put in a bit of time in Liverpool, or somewhere north, as a union organiser, and he wasn't shy about telling anyone that. I liked that about him. His sense of what was right. Beneath it all there was, had always been, a really smart man. The man with me now though was a bit of a beaten docket. And bitter. Yeah, there was that bitterness in everything he said. Those rugby mantras were just ironic incantations. Meant to gibe and to hurt, but they were weak and meaningless. Self-harm. Sad stuff really. He didn't reply, just sank his lips around another drink. Now he was getting drunk. I had a short window.

'I don't mean to upset you. I know what you are, Sean. Call it working class if you like, although it was more peasant back then. For everyone. But now. You, Sean. You are nothing if not working class yourself. Now. Right here. But what does that do for anyone? There are no heroes. Fuck John Lennon.'

'Yes... fuck him for sure... fuck the lot of them.' He was hitting the maudlin buttons too.

'But don't take it out on your brother. No matter what his... his jazz. He's sick, Sean. Maybe you should go and see him.'

He began the hiccupping routine.

'Gerry, you are a smart boy. Take me home alright. Home to Leicester Square... home to Wi-wig-an... home to... to Bal... Bal... aw fuck home... fuck Duh... Dub-lin. Is your mammy well? Take me home though. You will?'

'I will. I will Sean. I'll take you home.'

*

I didn't take him home that night. I just went back to the soaring axes at The Roundhouse. And Zeppelin. If you're going to get your head wrecked... I didn't see him in London again. I went back to Dublin before that year was out and got a job teaching. He never did visit my father but he phoned my mother occasionally. But not again after she let rip at him when he called her, drunk, one evening after my father died. She only ever hinted at what he had said.

*

I called him a few times after that but he was either not in, or he wouldn't take the call. The best part of twenty years passed before I knew much about Sean again. My mother was gone. So was Sean's sister in Mayo; he'd made a few furtive trips to her over the years but she wasn't wont to tell me much. I often thought of him as I made my own mind up about the world. Moya and I had got married and settled into what was fast becoming the Irish fat-cat republic. I was on the executive of my teachers' union and worked hard. One evening, the phone rang in our house in Fairview. Coins dropped at the calling end. It was an oldish voice asking if Gerry Gilvarry lived there. The London–Irish strains were unmistakeable.

'Yes that's me. Sean?' I said it with a little excitement. 'Is that you Sean?'

The voice at the other end waited, allowing me to settle.

'No. This isn't Sean. I'm sorry to have to tell you but Knocky... eh Sean has died.'

Another bit of a pause, allowing me to take it in before I enquired.

'Who's this?'

'I met you once, over on this side, with Sean. Tipperary. Dan Breen.'

I hadn't forgotten that Easter Sunday.

'Sure. Of course. Thanks for calling. That's very sad news. How are you keeping yourself?' As I waited, there was nothing to distinguish what might have been an answer from interference on the line. So I changed the question.

'How did you find me?'

Turned out they had remained good buddies and that Sean often spoke of me, so he traced me through directory enquiries.

'Knocky always said you promised to take him home.' Tipp had found his voice again.

'I did? I mean I did.' I could hear Sean's stuttering, drunken repetition of that request echoing through all the years. Told many times to this Tipperary man and who knows how many others. Sean's holding on. His grip.

'So what's the plan. He's in the morgue over at Wandsworth. You know they don't rush things here. Not like... at home...' He trailed off and we said our quiet goodbyes.

But 'at home'? That man must be away for over fifty years. 'At home'! Clearly I had a funeral to organise. It made me feel a bit happy.

*

It was a Good Friday and the jet roared up a mighty rumpus as it appeared beneath the low black ceiling of the sky. It gripped the runway on the boggy plateau and came towards us in a wail of engine vanes. Knock airport and the heavens had opened. It was bucketing down. The crew and a few passengers scuttled in as we waited under three black brollys. Moya, the kids, myself and the undertaker's man. A forklift appeared and went to a cargo door whose hydraulics had begun moving. Suddenly there it was, high on the forks: Sean's box. The forklift operator was in 'where do ye want it?' mode as he lined it up and I helped manhandle it into the dryness of the hearse. Moya placed some daffodils over the brass plate. I checked that the people 'over on the other side' had used the words I'd sent. They had. I pocketed a small package wrapped in plastic that had been taped to the box. That could wait. Now all we needed was to get down to the village and the church.

There was a small attendance at the funeral mass: the rotund, fumbling priest, a woman in a headscarf sitting beside a much older woman, also in a headscarf, and a few old men. The older woman cried. I remembered the Litany of the Saints. The village was grey with a splash of sodden primroses and daffodils. We got to the graveyard and the rain had stopped. The sky lightened to a dirty yellow. The two men who had opened the grave leaned on their shovels, their grubby shirts open at the cuffs and sacks over the shoulders of their filthy coats. There was a strange vacancy beneath their brows. One was short and stumpy, the other wasted-looking and lanky. They both tipped their caps to sympathise. We got the box down and the priest recited a fast decade of the rosary. We left to the slurping of the shovels and the spatter of pebbles on wood as the succulent Mayo earth was poured back around Sean. I opened the little package when we sat into the car. It contained an enamelled metal badge with the words 'Amalgamated Union of Building Trades Workers'.

Sean's union. It was wrapped in a newspaper cutting with a photograph of a silver-haired man. 'That's Nye Bevan.' Moya was emphatic, and she knew these things. There were pink streamers deepening in the sky to the west and that made me happy.

*

'Can we open an egg? Just one, pleee-ase?' our six-year-old boy, Sean-Óg, asked as we reached Athlone.

'Sssshh Sean. Dad tell us the story again about the Sean who was in the coffin and how he and grandad didn't say much to each other.' Katie, the older one, had been worrying about that. Moya raised her eyebrows and rolled the window down. I found the words I needed.

'Well you see Uncle Sean didn't like grandad's jazz that much and...'

'What's jazz?' Sean-Óg was busy unwrapping the gold paper from his egg.

'Well... it was some fancy stuff that Sean didn't like.' I was back in those nights in London. 'But he's home now. And that's what he wanted.'

'Why didn't he come home sooner then?' Katie sounded her most worried yet and, as we headed back east over the River Shannon, her big question found some muggy air in which to hang.

BIRDY

The Queen of the May stood stony and sunkissed above Christy, who read again the inscription at her feet: *Pray for all those who were lost to the sea.* There was something about the breeze-blown blossoms at the base of the statue that made him think of the spirits of the drowned. The bed was strewn with pink petals, and brown glass from a broken bottle. The rest of the world must find it peculiar, he reminded himself, how the fishermen don't learn how to swim.

It was his little one's First Communion and he wasn't welcome along. He had been shut out since just after Amy was born, when it was discovered that she was a little different. That set off the whole shebang. Kay, Amy's mother, was a Kinsella. No one messed with the Kinsellas. As a charity, he was allowed to work a quarter share on Mick Kinsella's trawler — Kay and the kid were off limits. Now and again there would be a sharp shot across the bows from Mick. It could happen over a quiet pint in the Pier, or at a pool table in the Jammer. It happened once during an aching, sodden haul to save a catch in a big blow. The wind had grabbed every word, so Mick couldn't be sure that Christy had understood the fresh warning. Mick was never the worst to him though; that job was for the other Kinsella brothers and, particularly, the sisters.

'I'd stay the fuck away Birdy, if it were me.'

These were Mick Kinsella's parting words yesterday when they had tied up at the quay and unloaded the boxes. So, when Christy slipped into the back of the church, he was on watch.

As a young lad, Christy Butler had not been run-of-the-mill. He was small, jerky and unpredictable, with all his energy stored, it seemed, in his coal eyes, which were hooded like a hawk's. When he was talking with you he squinted and, if you followed closely, his gaze would dart about, making the whole business uneasy. His voice was composed of burnt sounds that came direct from his throat. You'd more likely have found him blowing eggs that he'd taken from gulls' nests on the cliffs than in a classroom; or, as the years grew by, on his Honda 50, dressed in his denims, breezing along the coast road into Walton's music shop in the city when the other lads were kicking a ball. He loved his music—The Righteous Brothers 'Unchained Melody', he sang it to his 'love' — and wore Ban-the-Bomb insignia, which were in sharp contrast to his penchant for trapping and killing gulls. He reckoned they were vermin, as did his ma. He had sliced gulls as a child, before he ever took a blade to a cod. 'Birdy' they called him. He even began to imagine himself as a bird. Not like the gulls that cried behind the trawler when it chugged in laden with a catch; gulls, whose nests he had raided on the cliffs, whose guts he had spilled. No, he saw himself more like the peregrine he had watched gliding over the cliffs and then diving like a falling anchor. Nowadays, the Kinsellas regarded Christy as avian, and nothing else.

*

The church was packed. Standing at the back, he was okay. The families were all up towards the front. He nodded to a few of the older men and women that he knew and liked. They took him in and returned looks that said 'pity'. Everyone in this place was on terms and most were somehow related. Christy stood in a corner, near the candles at the shrine to Saint Jude, and searched through the throng of heads for the little white veils at the front. It could be today, he thought. It was impossible to see clearly, but he settled on a lacy head for Amy and waited. He would spot her for sure when she went up for the bread.

*

The Butlers had always been known for their afflictions: missing relatives, tics, rasping coughs, gunner eyes, callipers, leg braces, drawn curtains. For years, until she passed on, it had been just himself and his ma living together in the little terrace four-roomer that overlooked the harbour. Christy, like his da and his granda, had gone on the trawlers in traditional crews of hard men and loners like himself. This was a rough station of rolling boat decks and bars—long, tough hours at sea and the obliteration of drink ashore. Christy was, however, sharper than the rest in everything he did. He mostly avoided the pub, preferring to ride his motorbike into the city beat clubs while other lads angrily shifted their arses on barstools. He flitted about, at the edge of things, popping up with a laugh here and a clever word there. No one could hold his eye long enough to get inside his head. He was regarded as a bit of an oddball, but he had survived by playing a bit of a fool. He was able to hang in and stand out in the one breath and that's what had attracted Kay Kinsella to him. He started to take her to the clubs on the back of his motorbike and they had a kind of secret optimism together. Even though Kay was a Kinsella, as a sixteen-year-old she could still dream, and she began to dream for herself and Christy.

'We'll be away from all this, Christy Butler. You and me, we'll fly away from here.'

'Ah'll be packed and ready, kid. Now let's dance.'

Kay found out the hard way that escape needed a better plan than she had come up with. She had come up with Birdy Butler and the start of a baby. That kicked her dreams. When her family got hold of the news, they took over and encouraged the birdy-boy to be scarce. And Kay started to get in touch with the Kinsella in herself. That was nothing though, compared with the vileness after the little one was born. That's when the real misery began for Christy 'Birdy' Butler. The air thickened with anger and accusation. There was talk of some disorder in his family. Blame the Butlers. He began sneaking about, watching and being watched. He tried to follow Amy's progress but no one was talking, no one who knew. He would drop into Peggy Mooney's bar. Peggy was his ma's old pal.

'Peggy, they are saying it's the Butler blood is bad, got poisoned over the years. There's no badness in that little girl, whatever is the matter with her. I don't even know what it is though, 'cos they won't let me next nor near her.'

'I know, Christy, and it's a shame. That little thing needs her father.'

'Did I tell you that I met her on the quay, one day we were in early? She was with Kay and I'm telling you, she knew who I was. Her eyes opened up in the biggest smile for me, just so beautiful. I'd be a good da for her.'

'You'd be a great father for her if they'd only let you. But you know those people, son. That family is where the wickedness is. You'll just have to let it go for now. Who knows what the next tide might bring?'

Every time he did catch a glimpse of his little girl, the feeling was unbearable, so he tried to just ride it, like a rogue wave. More and more he became a tomb for his own pain. All his peculiar energies flickered and burned.

'I'm tired of it all, Peggy.'

*

The priest was standing, all hopeful looking, holding up the host, as the little line started to shift towards him. Christy strained at the profiles: there, I have her now, the little beauty, he thought. His eyes didn't stray as the tiny thing edged along the row, all serene and pretty. He was humming his Righteous Brothers' love melody, suddenly got all jiggly and nudged the old man beside him, not meaning to. 'Ah, Austy, I'm sorry about that. It's... ah... my little girl... up there. Look. Isn't she a picture?'

Austy Fogarty wouldn't see ten feet out, so it made no odds, but he could smell, and he got a warm waft of whiskey filtered through a perfume of burning wax.

'She is that, Christy... a beautiful little girl.'

After the ceremony, in the throng outside, Amy looked peaky. Goose bumps on her skinny legs; a shiver in white, in an early summer shower. 'Queen of the angels,' Christy whispered to himself as he hung back and waited for a signal. Let it be today of all days. The trembling Kinsella sisters gaggled about her. Granny, Ma Kinsella, was all queen too, in her new hat, looking severely now in his direction. A lady on point duty, with the cavalry behind — best hold your hour now, he thought. He got his sign from Amy when her moist stare found his. Somehow, nothing broke their connected gaze as he pushed his way over and reached in to hand her the little package. Even the phalanx of Kinsella chiffon and flesh parted for him.

'Here, darling, I've kept that for you. It was your Gran Butler's.'

He wanted to kneel beside her, but he thought that maybe he would be better just to hold the ground he had already made. As she opened the box, he looked down on her tiny, crowned head, and the sweet scents that wafted up started his tears. She held the silver ring and chain in the pearly fingers of her gloves and looked up at him. At first he saw only into her eyes, and the eternity that was held there; then her smile that came from some other place.

'Thanks Birdy.'

All the eyes in the churchyard were on them. He choked, his words like cinders.

'You look great. Love you.'

'Thanks.' She whirled away. 'Ma, look what Birdy gave me.'

That was enough, Kay's cold stare told him, before the ranks closed. The looks from Mick Kinsella and his brothers, in their suits over at the grotto railing, told him too. Mick gave a shrug that said, I told you so.

Kay's place was small, so there was a party up at Ma Kinsella's. Not for Christy, though. His thoughts all a confusion, he settled for the pub. He stayed on his own in the bar and raised his whiskey to a crowd visible across the counter, in the lounge. A couple of the younger lads nodded back. They would've called him Birdy, he

figured. Later, Austy would say that they'd talked over a
few drinks and that, at first, Christy was pretty agitated.
'As you'd expect,' he said, 'given the circumstances.'

'D'you know, Austy, when you'd be out and the
wind would get up strong and you'd be just bouncing
around, you know, waiting to see what it would do? Before you'd put anything out? Or head in? You know that
time, it can go either way and you'd better be ready?'

'I know what you're saying okay. Or if you had them
out, and you needed to cut and run, eh? That'd be when
your skipper would earn his share.'

'I was just thinking of that very thing earlier.
You know I always had this lad ready to do just that.'
Christy pulled back the flap of his suit jacket to show
Austy the knife in the waistband. 'Cut bone, that edge.'

'Begor, Christy, it would and all. Cut a thick line
that would.'

'Yeh, Austy, cut a lot of thickness, it sure would.
Sometimes I think... sometimes... ah you know I used
to think I'd get myself away from here... this place.
Now it's like... you must know this... it's like an open
grave, everywhere you look... out there... on shore...
and you're in it every day... can't climb out. Dug for you
the day you were born. Sure look at the graveyard where
it is, sitting there in the middle of us all... looking in
everyone's window.'

'It's there, Christy, for it to be close to the souls
out at sea.'

'Waiting for us, land or sea. You're a decent man,
Austy, and long may you stay above ground. I need to be
out of here now.'

'Take it handy, Christy.'

Austy'd been concerned about him, as the lad wasn't normally a big drinker, but he thought that he'd seemed more focused as he headed away.

Up the hill, Peggy Mooney served him a couple of pints in her front snug and sold him whiskey to take out. She said he left sometime after nine. She'd found him upset and he'd cried. They'd talked about his mother. Vera used come into Peggy before she lost her husband. (Christy's da, Dinny, had gone down with the Ave Maria — seven good men in a sunken coffin.) Christy'd been very sad, and a little drunk, and she'd thought he'd just go home, with a little comfort, and sleep it away.

'A terrible hard day for him though. I mean what were they at, keeping him away from that poor little child? He said he was tired and couldn't face anybody. I told him to go on off home. Forget about it all for today, Christy Butler, I told him. Sure they had the poor man tormented.'

Ma Kinsella's place was littered with bottles, paper plates and plastic forks. A bucket load of coleslaw had been consumed. A blur in white to her mother and everyone else, Amy had her cousins to mind her, and they swarmed about from room to room and into the garden, giddy on lemonade. She was allowed to take off her veil, but her little bag had never left her wrist.

Around ten in the evening she said that she wanted to have a rest and went to her Granny's room on her own. She switched on the bedside lamp, settled on the bed and spilled the contents of her bag onto the faded quilt. It was mostly notes, coins and holy medals but there was one small creamy coloured box. She took out the ring on the chain. She thought it was beautiful and went to the window to see a reflection of it hanging round her little neck. But that wasn't all she saw in the windowpane. Christy was in the window too. His red-flecked, emaciated, bearded features, black squinty eyes and blistered lips were somehow there, with her. Their images frozen together in a frame, for the first time. Amy and her da. Christy with Amy, his daughter. Before she could take it all in, there was a commotion and two of her aunts were in the room with her. Shadows were outside the window, shouting. She could hear her uncles' angry voices. She remembered that sweet smell she'd got from their breaths earlier.

'He's gone into the hedge. I'll go round, you go in.'

'Come out, Birdy, you fecker... you dirty fecker... you were told.'

Amy came back into the living room with her aunts. The party had changed. Now everyone was standing up, talking loudly. Her mother was crying and being held by Granny and other aunts. Uncle Mick was looking furious. Another uncle rushed in the door.

'Someone call an ambulance for Paddo. He's stabbed and pumping. Quick, hurry. We're getting out the cars. Birdy's heading up for the cliffs. We'll cut him off.'

Amy put her shivering arms around her mother's waist and was wrapped by aunties.

There were several paths through the gorse and Christy knew them, like he knew an old board game. He was calm, but moving fast, and the night was still. Behind him there had been the vivid cones of head-lights and the menace of engines. Now it was just the confused beams of torches and weaker shouts. He could hear his name being called, distant and echoing faint-ly, over and over.

'Birdy. We'll get you, Birdy... you little bollix... you were always a little bollix, Birdy.'

There was no chance now that any of them would catch up on him tonight, not in this dark. He would beat them to it. To his left, out in the vast blue-black, beyond the cliffs, was the sea. He found the path down that he was looking for and felt even safer. The hunting noises had tapered off — as he reckoned they would. The Kinsellas had stayed higher and were headed for the old Martello fort—a place that reeked of shit and piss.

The night-blue sky lit his way as he stepped on, his footing sure and steady; this was his ground. The gorse dropped off and he came into a clearing of wind-blown grass, a high meadow. He stripped himself of his blood-splattered clothes. The grass brushed softly against his naked body as he climbed the gradual rise towards a high horizon in the stars. Moving his toes from grass to clay, pebble by pebble, he felt his way to the edge. He knew when to stop.

Hundreds of feet below him a mournful sea was heaving relentlessly. In one glance, Christy united it all with the heavens. He was now a lonely silhouette with arms outstretched, feeling for a draught. Birdy. He could hear his own low sounds, his breathing, his humming. His mouth and throat dry in the high air. A dog yapped somewhere, far off. Must be from one of the posh houses higher up. They had some view, he thought, but all they ever notice is the sails.

'Bet you they can swim,' he shouted.

He waited for the echo and then, releasing all bone, he was diving, falling like an anchor.

A SIGNAL DISORDER

It was over fifty years since Shea had fallen out of the world. A wiry, dark-featured presence up in Lacey's old tumbledown place. Back then he was 'on the run from the North', had 'come back from the African missions'—whatever dismal notion his desperate look inspired. But he was none of that, nor was he a Greek — 'a fugitive from the Colonels' — who the late schoolmaster Johnson had jokingly called Pluto (no-one understood that, whichever way it was explained). He had moved in with his suitcase, his transistor radio and the accent that nobody could quite get a handle on—not that he ever said much. The place was barely habitable so the rent didn't amount to a whole lot, and there was regular money into the post office, with the whisper that it was *from America*. It was in Philomena Hynes's time as postmistress and her whisper could corrode the hinge of any secret. The Guards were around to check him out — nothing. He'd even got a licence for a gun — he had Lacey's permission — for rabbits and vermin. He knew how to use the gun too. Sometimes the only sign of him for weeks was the scatter of rooks from the trees after a loud crack. A story started doing the rounds about him sleeping out in the same trees with only the crackle of the transistor for company. There was truth in that.

A few years after he first landed-up, Shea's mother died somewhere — he didn't go, as there was some mix-up over his own whereabouts and things had gotten confused. It was the first time anyone from anywhere else had come looking for him. When they tracked him down, there were weeds growing on top of her. Some years after that again, he had another visitor. A black American man. By all accounts a disturbed young man, whose father apparently had something to do with Shea. He'd stayed a night in bed and breakfast accommodation nearby. Very little was revealed, but maybe enough to suggest that Shea was guilty of something more than his abandonment of the world. It was said that Shea had barricaded himself against the boy. He had, in fact, sealed up so tight that when the next day came, the boy didn't return. All that was long ago now and there hadn't been any word since, that anyone knew about. But that last visit had caused a shift in the local wariness about him. It was like there was now a reason to let him be. Although what that was, no-one could really say. And so it was that he was feared and protected at the one time.

*

Brady the postman broke off from conversations with a feigned concoction of concern and surprise, in order to be on his way. He liked most people and ragged easily with them. There were a few though, as he put it himself, he had an 'avarsion to'. He would have had a great feeling of discomfort if, in her day, he needed Philomena Hynes's signature — she had never learnt the simple grace of anything. So too when he had to drag himself with the parcel up to Shea's place at the edge of Lacey's Wood. He was coming out of a sweltering high-noon in July — it hadn't spilled a drop for three weeks. Shea's gate mechanism seemed to lack any working hinges and to find new places for sticking and scraping every time it was asked to function. It was not unlike Shea himself whose name had even lost a hinge — his name was Brendan O'Shea but, in the way that letters and such went astray, it had become the barer, harsher version. Of course interruption was not to Shea's liking (nor was anything that anyone wanted to know about him) and he stood now, in his grubby shirt-sleeves, set in the peeling frame of the door with his baleful look, like a bad dog. As old 'Hippo' Grainger used say, 'Shea don't need no doggy, he does his own growlin' and bitin'.'

The shack beyond was a low affair dwarfed by gigantic tumbles of parched-looking ragwort and honeysuckle and other wild shrubs that swarmed and hid everything below the twisted guttering and the flaky red tin roof. Brady handed over the package and followed Shea's dangerous eyes as they examined the address. Both men stood as if waiting for some recognition: that say, this was in fact a delivery, or some such thing that might be ready to be completed. Shea harrumphed and held the parcel exactly as it had been placed in his hands. Brady felt the bony-man's scan of his own round softness. The sight of the beleaguered duty-man's sweaty mouth seemed to provoke in Shea the need of some response, and in any case he tipped out the phlegm that had been heating up inside him. He cleared his lungs and spat.

'Shocking hot. What the fuck's a man to do?'

Brady felt a trickle of damp release between his shoulder blades. He couldn't understand how this tossed-about looking man could come over so dark and frightening. It was all in his eyes he reckoned. And he, Brady, and all the rest of them did have a great fear of Shea, a man still very much come out of the blue despite all those years holed up in this place. And more hidden away you couldn't get around there. And that suited everyone.

'That's for you so?' Brady needed only not to have it refused.

'Funny thing. Funny okay,' Shea growled and still held the package in a kind of no-man's territory with not a trace of light about him. He went on in his slow drawl. 'I was only thinking the other day that some bastardin' thing...' He appeared to run out of steam but he was still thinking, obviously.

Brady himself was thinking 'why can't you just say it to fuck?' But he tried for something a little better. 'It's properly addressed. Someone knows you still.' And then in a grasp at some sort of a connect. 'Hear you ran the phone company out of it again.' Then he gave it another go. 'It looks like it's from America.'

A sudden grimace found its way into Shea's features. He darkened even more and then seemed to stagger. After some seconds of watching, Brady was moved to concern.

'You okay?'

Shea opened his eyes and resumed his usual bleak pose.

'America? Oh yes. They've tried coming here. Sent signals. They have. No, I was saying to myself... No, it's me. America.' And he dropped his hands, the brown package in his right grip and sighed. 'What do I... something or other... how—'

'Nothing, it's all sorted. You mind yourself, do you hear.'

And Brady was off, without any sound, not knowing what he had just said and leaving the gate somewhat closed. Off to empty out the rest of his day as quickly as he could.

Shea settled in the coolness by the tiny north window and looked at the parcel. His name was written in big confident letters 'Brendan O'Shea' and the address was more or less right. He saw it was a U.S. stamp and was sure there was something familiar about the writing. The package was padded with some sort of stuffing. He opened it, and out came a lilac coloured envelope and a small bundle of hard things wrapped in transparent plastic with little blisters of air pockets. He started a bit when he first felt the hardness, and then he froze to look at it, but didn't want to touch it again. After a while he relaxed enough to set it aside and he opened the envelope. In it was a family photograph taken outside a suburban house somewhere in the United States: a black family—what looked like a mother, a father and three children. The young father held a framed photograph of another young black man in a smart uniform; they all looked out like they were making some sort of an appeal. Like you would for a missing person. The flag of the stars and stripes hung on a pole. He squinted to read the handwriting on the back of the photograph.

*

Cora Braiden was a woman who had been coming to see him over a good few years, and who he had begun to call his 'nurse'. She was, in fact, a social worker. He'd considered that the whole business of her visits might have been a complete mistake in the first place, given that he had never asked for anything. He'd offered no welcome when she'd first appeared and told him: 'I got a note from the Welfare that you were living alone here, so we thought it no harm to drop by now and again and see how you were doing.'

He hadn't turned down the cassette-player, which was blaring out a scratchy-thin version of The Doors' 'Riders on the Storm'.

'That squelch. Insane.' He'd muttered and then turned up the bass volume so she had to strain over the crisp electric riff to hear his response. 'I'm thrown down fine here. Fine if that's what you'd like to say. Put that down. You don't need to come... you know.' And then he'd muttered, 'What the fuck would you know anyway. Go away and listen to some music.'

But she had come back again, and then came a fair bit more. He didn't bother to listen to her when she sounded off about forms and reports and the like, but she seemed kind enough to him when her chatter found its more demotic courses. She would ask if he was eating and if he had fuel. Shea didn't bother to join any dots, he just accepted her as some sort of a well-meaning emissary from the world. She called him Brendan and brought him books and magazines from the library; he liked history books and *The National Geographic*. He hoped that she might be a farmer's wife with better things to be doing. His hope was near enough on the money, but he'd keep her at it anyway. He'd ask her things, say something about cats. 'Is there any truth that a person can get the Aids from a cat? I feed them you know. The big ones. They come out of that jungle out there.'

She would laugh at his questions but give him his answers, and then there might be a bit more natter about cats or jungles or whatever. There was only so long she could stay in the intensity with him — her eyes could not latch onto his for much more than a glance at a time — before she might have to leave. As far as he was bothered, she was welcome back anytime she wanted to shoot-the-breeze about cats or his 'rations' or indeed any old thing. For a man who was thought to enjoy only his own company and live so without much talking, he was happy enough now and again to hear the detail in an ordinary conversation, but damned if he always seemed to listen or understand, or not, what the half of it meant.

But Cora Braiden was figuring him out slowly. One day he announced that he was from down in West Kerry, but had spent time in the U.S. 'In the Sixties, way before your time', and had then gone on to mumble something about 'the hell of it all' and that set him off into a disturbance, and there wasn't a whole lot else he would say about it. She reminded him about the music he had been listening to the first day she came.

'The Doors. That sounds like "hell" music? I've listened to it you know.'

Out of nowhere he stood up and barked out the words 'RTO O'Shea. Americals. Killers on that road. Oh yeah, we made them squirm. Oh yeah. Did our own squirmin' then. Yessir, everyone squirmed in Kham Duc. Vee-et-Naam.' Then he began, in a conspiratorial whisper, to explain something about 'the red warning signals flashing, fucking with my head' and not being able to get the 'prick of a radio transmitter' to work; that 'it would be fucking too late when they got here.'

She had tried to come back to all that a few times but he would only get upset, and so she just left it. She was getting a picture of his 'hell' nonetheless. She had heard of Vietnam, but whatever she was figuring she was keeping it to herself. Cora Braiden liked something in the tone of this old Brendan, but she feared for his mind.

*

She'd come one day soon after the parcel had been delivered. 'That's a nice looking photograph you have there on the dresser, Brendan.' She moved closer to it and then backed away again moving her head in a pattern that floated from side to side. 'Their eyes look like they are following you. Was that man... in the uniform... is that the... the boy holding it?'

Shea signalled her to be silent and got himself up and went over and took the package in the bubble-wrap out of a drawer. He stood for a few moments to examine it, and then gestured that she might take it. It was still wrapped, undisturbed, as it had come. She took it and looked at him. 'So? What do you want?' she said. He gave one of those despairing looks he used when he was agitated, like he just didn't know whether to pull a trigger or not. Then he whispered in a quiet, defeated voice, 'what is it?' She opened the wrapping and laughed, but he didn't laugh with her and held the hopeless look. He fiddled anxiously with his hands, shifted onto a chair.

'Oh my god. You don't know, do you? My dear man, it's a phone. A mobile phone.'

He stopped his fidgeting and his eyes shifted into a neutral kind of mouldering.

'Can't for the life of me understand what they want me to do with the damned thing. What to do with the damned thing,' he repeated in a slow fearful cadence matched to the reluctance he had with the contraption.

She offered to help him get it up and running. Suddenly, just when she had it unwrapped and was pressing buttons, he leapt to his feet and shouted, 'Leave it. Just leave it.'

'Okie-dokie,' Cora sighed.

Then when she noticed that he seemed to be having a silent argument with the photograph on the dresser, she joined him in his long wordless disputation until a fear came on her and it was time to take her leave.

*

A week later she was back at his door. It was pouring down and she adopted an impatient tone, matching the intent in his eyes with her own.

'Brady said you wanted me to drop by.'

She had on a clear plastic raincoat with a hood that was so tight to her head that the rain ran down in rivulets over her face and made her look even more wholesome. He held the door half-open and himself back in the gloom. There was complete blackness to him: his eyes, his stubble, smoke from the grate of smouldering turf draping him. He just stood there in a silent sootiness, looking at her as if to say, 'Can I trust you?'

'Here I am so,' she said, not looking at all joyful about the prospect of being invited in, but preferring it to getting any more soaked.

She was in and drying and he was at the kettle before he spoke. 'Can you get that yoke going for me?'

The phone was laid out on the table with the various wires and attachments.

There was a gleam of damp on the faded blue and green oil-cloth. 'Sure.'

She went at it pretty fast and reached beyond him to the socket beside the kettle to get the charge going. She sat down and he moved about slowly getting cups and milk and a few biscuits. She didn't look at him or say anything.

'Sugar?' he asked and as usual she said 'No'.

'Tell me if there's maybe any sweetness in that though?' he said softly and threw the photograph face up in front of her.

She felt his tarry form passing behind her as he moved to sit at the opposite side of the table. He indicated with some movements of his head that she should turn the photograph over. She started to read. The writing was tight and urgent. It was headed with a date from about a month previously and started 'Dear Brendan...'

'So, you have someone who wants to forgive you. Someone called Alvin.'

Cora was trying to imagine something, maybe something very bad. The fact that it had all come from such a distance and seemed so intimate.

'He wants to forgive you,' she repeated. 'So he wants you to use the phone. That's okay, isn't it?' She watched a confusion come against the refusal in his eyes.

Shea was thinking of *a graveyard somewhere, with flags blowing*. Then he was hearing *a loud mechanical noise*; he was seeing himself *in a circle of blazing grass and he was so frozen; he was clinging onto a large radio-transmitter that he couldn't remember how to use. The noise was now deafening.* On the inside of his eyelids a signal was glowing red. And it hit him that *he hadn't wanted to remember how to use it.* How could he consider these intimacies that he

knew nothing about anymore? When there was so much...
What made anyone who had been only a child then, and
lucky to be born where he was, want to drag all this up?

As far as Cora could see, Brendan O'Shea was
searching for something like permission, so she went
for the push. 'Let's see if this works.'

Outside, she got a weak signal and saw that there
was some credit. He followed her out. There was just one
number in the contacts. A long number. U.S. code. She
showed him how to call, stood back and left him to it.

A number of impulses played hard on him. He
fumbled with the phone and stayed in the one spot, as
Cora had suggested, to keep the signal. He could think
of nothing to say even though his head flooded like a
reservoir. Through the trees he saw a strip of a very
lush field beyond a cut-stone wall. The grass was gold
and bright. It held all the intensity of the sun. Was that
smoke coming in? And the *noise* from the sky. The trees
began to move. He felt some familiar urgency when he
made an effort to press the buttons like he'd been told.
He was thinking only of *call signs*, but he managed it. He
held the phone to his ear just as Cora had. The dial tone
was drowned out by an utterly familiar sound above the
trees. *Chopper blades.* It was hurting his ears. Finally it
all faded.

A man's voice said, 'Yes?'

'Brendan.' Shea spoke at the phone.

Brendan O'Shea held the minute apparatus tight
to his smudgy skull as he listened to the voice coming
and going. He remembered the meaning of *squelch*. *The
chopper came slashing back over.* He could just about make

out some words. He knew who this man was — a man who shouldn't ever forgive him for being alive. Maybe he had to forgive himself first. Or the man's father? Who was to forgive who here? This man, the son of a killer — his old man a murdering saviour like saint fucking Brendan here himself. Murderer. No different to the English bastards chopping into the continental papists in the Cutting Field, back in West Kerry all those centuries ago. And then the French, themselves in Vietnam, the trampling boots on their feet now, doing the slicing. After that, these *Americals*. Now they had come looking for him again. Was it in time, this time, or would they, or could he... this time? It seemed to him this line, or whatever it was, was never ending. They would come again, always come for him again and find him too late. And he, Shea, clockless and dateless, would go on having only the damage that was himself and having really *failed*. The signal always *red*. Failed to stop it all. And then failed to save them all. He listened and then said flatly, 'We can all be forgiven so. I'll send you my heart.' Before the line failed and was reduced to a static buzz.

'To hell with it again so,' he shouted and Cora took a step towards him. 'To hell with Radiotelephone Operators. Vietnam. *Americals my hole, Sir!*'

He grasped her in one of his stares and stopped shouting. Then his look changed to a sort of appeal, like in the photograph of the family, and he started to talk away urgently, like he was giving evidence.

'I didn't want to get that prick of a set to work... get that signal out... to get those big birds in, in time to save that fucked-up... that Alvin's old man and the others. Blue... that's what he was called. Blue Curtis. Too fucking late. The killing still in his eyes. That was my job and I couldn't even do it. A fucking Irish saint with a radio-pack on his back. Trying not to save us bastardin' child-murderers. Yeah, the killing still in our eyes. And the hate — wherever that came from,' he rattled on, his voice rising again. 'The fucking cavalry came too late for him... but got me out. Oh yes me. Oh yes, saved me to face the music. And the boy who came to punish me, now wants to forgive me? He might have saved his own father then. And finished me off. Fuck all that!'

Cora was about to say something when he rushed past her into the house. She heard him rustling about in the hallway and then the back door slamming. There were a couple of minutes silence as she pushed through the overgrowth at the side of the house to see what he was up to. Suddenly there was the loud crack of a gunshot followed by the noise of scattering rooks and a deathly silence that rooted her to the spot. Then she panicked and rushed on to the back of the house. She found him slumped against a tree with the gun slung low, relaxed, in his hands. The phone was on the ground at his feet. Still buzzing, it seemed to play out a dimmed version of an electric piano riff on a Doors' track. The rustled leaves above were settling and the memory of those riffs gorged in her head. There was a horrifying grin on his face and a paleness to him which made her cry out, but at the same time she had never seen a look on him that better resembled something that he might have actually wanted to feel. He was whispering calmly, 'Forgive me so. I forgive you. I will send you my hero's heart.'

It seemed almost promising—but only if she could get her own cavalry in on time.

*

'Thanks for posting that on. My Purple Heart. All those years you've been coming. All that time that I didn't even know your name. Thank you, Cora. You're good at the signals. I was thinking of getting the phone in.'

'Sure what would you need it for? Who in the hell would you ever want to talk with?'

It was some months later and Cora Braiden was looking into bright eyes in a hopeful, freshly shaven face. There were no smears of black and the deep lines were clean. Inside the house it was brighter too, since the bushes had been cut back. The room was ordered with new things: a coffee machine, a digital clock, a new stereo and a microwave oven. This new man shrugged pleasantly and said, 'There's a good few in their hells, Cora, could call me if they want. There's many came back here to this country. We could talk. Maybe I'll call them.'

There was a silence to ease the bones.

'Hell's Angel. That's who I'll be. What was it someone called me? When I came here first. Pluto? Good name that. I'll keep it too. Better than some Irish saint trying to squeeze more pain from his heart. Anyway, I've let that off to him. But I'll hang on to the gun; let off the odd round, to keep the bad spirits at bay.'

He made an almost happy sound.

Cora looked out beyond him at the communications mast on the distant hill. There was a flashing red light on the top. Shea caught her attention and she turned to him. They locked eyes. And a few moments later the smiles arrived. And with that, his softest words.

'Haven't you better things to be doing now? Over there with your farmer?'

Then he went and turned up the sound on the new stereo. It played a Beethoven symphony. He turned to her and, still smiling, raised his voice to one of its edgier pitches.

'And by the way, Jim Morrison did have something about him too, you know.'

NIGHT MUSIC

There he was, a priest in the sun, like an actor on his mark. He looked away, effacing, as if to say, 'I have you', from the start. '*I* have *you*', I thought.

I'd just guided the stylus onto the first track and as the scratchy hum from the speakers confirmed contact, I heard a faint rap on the front door. Who in this wilderness had come calling? I silenced the sounds, wiping the first bars of Miles Davis's *Kind of Blue* from the air, and went to see. Outside in the August haze was a shrivelled-looking creature all in faded black. His pursed lips threatened to whistle or begged of thirst. Nothing else in his face stood out from a desperate wanness. The delicate head was balanced on a narrow contortion of skin and pipe that slipped through a stiff yellowing collar without fuss. Why didn't it choke them? And all their medieval repression? Need to make martyrs of us all. The concealed body was, no doubt, lacerated and pierced, like Sebastian? I needed shot of this intruder. Get back to the glory of my man on the turntable.

'How can I help you?' says I.

'Oh,' says he, 'aren't those little flowers just beautiful?'

'Gladioli. For *respect* they say.' I watched the snowy cat pop her nose around the blistered green gate.

'A sight,' he offered. 'This blessed earth.'

The cat squeezed herself under the bottom rung of the gate and padded towards the geranium pots, the audience taking her seat. She settled there and took us both in: the nanny-goat priest and myself, the young fella that fed her.

'Yeh, blessed with human care. Can I help you at all?'

'Oh yes, your sign "Cabbage plants for sale".'

'Yeh, they're round the back... in a bed... late plants. Yorks. English I'm afraid.'

I could smell the heat off the straw roof a foot above my head and I wanted to move this along, so I led on through the yard and into the side garden, by the gap in the privet hedge. He overcame his inclination to go first and found a gait that tried to say authority, but just about coaxed a shuffle that kept up behind me. I could sense the cat follow us by a series of creature shortcuts. As I passed by the corner of the house, I opened the tap that fed into a yellow hose. The sun blazed on the vegetable patch. The blue-green cabbage plants were collapsed, splayed imploringly on the cakey soil.

'They'll be in need of a drink,' says I, 'but they're fine.'

'Do you take a drop yourself?' He was now doing a wringy-hand type thing and giving me a crotchety look. I wondered if he would suddenly pull out a pamphlet; something with the dark shadow of a man in despair on the cover.

'I like a pint.' I checked my level of civility. 'And yourself?'

'You are new around, yourself. Dublin, is it?'

'Yeh Dublin. I'm here three, four months. Happy enough. So far. Good to be away from the Smoke.'

'Is it? Very?'

'What?'

'Smokey?'

'Oh no, that's what we call Dublin. The city. I suppose it is. In the winter.'

'You can have as much smoke as you want here. As long as it's legal. Light a fire, you know. You'll get a bit of turf? The winters can be cold.'

'Yeh, I'm hoping for a simpler life. Easier to heat and all legal.'

'Oh sure it's a great community here. To move into. Rural people. Quiet people. Mind their own business.'

'Quiet. Sure. Well, I find them marvellous. Friendly. Helpful. I've good neighbours. Peg, Ned.'

'Not ours.'

'Sorry?'

'They'd be Church of Ireland. Ned and Peg. The McConnells. Estate people.'

'Oh, I see what you mean. Well, sure that's a fact so.'

I saw the little blaze that his eyes had become; fiery little windows to... what? I moved around the other side of the cabbage-bed, reversing places, to get at the hose, and got him in my shadow. I opened the faucet at the end of the hose and the warm water hissed and spluttered onto the bed. There was something helpless, yet dangerously unpredictable about this man who now stood silently, watching me watering cabbage plants. The only sound was from the water plipping into the dry soil. I could sense the cabbages revive as the ground dampened. I wondered if I should try and revive this priest with a splash or two.

'They'll perk up grand when you get them replanted. How many will I give you?'

He'd moved again, blocking the sun. I held up my palm for shade as I tried to find his eyes. All I could see was the sun exploding from his head on top of his black form. His features danced into focus, x-rayed, and I saw that his eyes, like dark beads from a rosary, helpless in their shell holes, were staring back up at the cottage. I repeated, 'So, how many?'

He turned back towards me. 'Ah, let me see. A shilling's worth?'

That was old currency now, but I plucked a couple of dozen of the frail plants from the wet soil and bunched them. I held them up, damp clay clinging to the tangle of translucent roots, for his inspection. He paid no heed. He was clearly not too interested in buying cabbage. He looked hot and bothered. I started back towards the cottage.

'Grand so. I'll get some newspaper.'

Something stirred in a part of me. A sudden sympathy? I turned back to him.

'Maybe you'd like a drop of something? Above in the cottage? We can get out of this sun.'

He followed me without a word, in under the baking stems of the eaves, and I showed him into the end room and offered him one of the wooden-backed chairs. The room was alive with music from the stereo I had turned up: jazz from Miles. The sun clipped the reveal of the window to the rear, but a curtain was drawn to keep out the direct glare from the side window. Soon the faint shadow of the cat settled itself on the sill outside. The atmosphere in the room was peachy soft and my visitor seemed to soften too as soon as he sat. I wrapped the plants in newspaper and left them on the dresser. I pulled a bottle of Black Label from the old pine cupboard and held it up. He nodded his approval and I lifted two glasses in the fingers of my other hand. I thought of him washing his fingers in water from a cruet (his eye on the other cruet with his wine) during the altar ceremony as I placed the glassware on the scrubbed boards of the table in front of my man. I'm sure I saw his nostrils flare.

'He is one of the lucky ones.' He nodded toward the stereo and finished the statement with his glass tipped into his mouth.

'Miles? Lucky? He's a junkie.'

He drained the glass and gazed at me for a moment.

'Was. He had such a long respite, 'til recently, wherever he's holing up. A great word that. Junkie. Sure aren't we all junkies of one sort or another?' This sounded like a sermon. 'I am a fan of American jazz music.'

Where was this coming from? This priest that had been withering in the sun earlier was plumping up.

'I thought you people called it "devil's music"?'

'Oh, I've no doubt that some do. People call us things too you know. But no, I am a... an aficionado, I believe is the word I am looking for. Hawkins. Tatum. Bebop. Charlie Bird Parker was my all-time hero. Unlucky Bird. Do you play anything at all yourself?'

'Drums, just a bit. Rock. A little keyboard, not so well.'

'You see I play a little myself. Piano. Not much jazz. Oh no, not in the parochial. It's Chopin and Schubert all the way there. But in my youth... yes. And the occasional little... outing... still. Every man has his holidays, and a few weekends you know. Oh yes, little hobbies. There's a good few follow the horses, National Hunt you know. And the doggies.' His voice dropped into a whisper. 'A fellow PP I know down in Cork goes to Brands Hatch and rides heavy motorbikes. And for another man I know, it's Milan for the Opera.'

'Normal is what you are saying?'

'No, more than normal. Ordinariness is for small minds.'

'But yours, your flock, what are they?'

'Ordinary people, yes. Their intelligence is of a collective nature. There is nothing small about faith.'

The desiccating priest from earlier now had traces of a glow in his veins. His arms moved more freely. He crossed and uncrossed his legs as he warmed to his thoughts. His fingers tapped rhythms to my only Charlie Parker album, which now did its thirty-three and a third revolutions per minute. He gave me his hardest look yet and I sensed a different dryness off him as he spoke again.

'Great music, and literature, is good for the soul. Needed for the soul.'

'You respect modern expression then?'

'Of course. Modern, whatever's after that. Labels. It's the individuals that matter. Proust. Eliot. Joyce. Beckett.'

'Might hold on there. Wasn't Joyce on the...?'

'Sure, of course he was. That started in America. With the postal service. He was a wonderful writer. Not easy. You like the Russians?' He lifted *Fathers and Sons* from the table and glanced at the books stacked on the dresser.

'Yes, I'm a big fan. It's a relief from all that heavy American Beat and druggy stuff. Burroughs. But I suppose all that's good with you, fits in with the jazz? I much prefer the humanity of the Russians.'

'Pre-modernist. Pre-revolution. Ah where did all that humanity get them?'

This conversation had gone a long way from the cabbage patch in the sun. He had become almost frisky. I was interested, but I got a peculiar feeling that I was being cornered. In fairness, several peculiar thoughts went through my mind as I tried to figure this priest out. Better slow him down first I reckoned, or he would have me out of my depth. I offered to top him up. I thought let's go that way and see if we can get this on to a different ground. Let him try and mark out his real territory there. And me mine.

'So, you are the boss-man of the church in these parts?'

'More the boss-man's man I would say. You are not a believer?'

'You've drawn that conclusion. Why?'

'Young man, down from the city, seeking out the simple country life. Listens to serious music, reads serious books. You say "yours" to me. No, I'd say you've no time for my faith.'

'I'm not a hippy if that's what you think. Not that decadent.'

'Another wonderful word that. Your Russians would call jazz decadent.'

'My Russians are all dead. And the new ones don't think jazz is decadent. Not anymore. Not for years.'

'We are all in the same game. Trying to de-muddle peasant minds.'

'Or keep them muddled. Isn't that safer?'

I'd turned the radio on to catch more music and now it was News time. The death of Elvis Presley was announced. An extraordinary thing then happened. My man was on his feet in the centre of the room. The feet were planted firmly, his spindly black legs twisting to a beat. He held an imaginary microphone in one liver-spotted hand and stretched to the ceiling beams with the other. Skull down, wisps of hair shaken out, he twanged out a version of 'Heartbreak Hotel', hitting the words with all the passion his frail body could muster and finding that 'lonely' place with a particular ease. I watched this strange priest give an astonishing evocation of the tragic man from Tupelo, until I was interrupted by the shrill tone of the phone ringing in the hallway. It was the woman from the local exchange telling me my brother'd been on earlier and offering to put in a call back to him. No doubt he'd called to talk about Elvis. As I chatted with her about the stunning weather, my priest went by me, departing with a shake of his raised hand, and disappeared into the dazzling broil. After I'd finished making the arrangements with the operator to return the call to my brother, I left down the receiver and heard the engine of his car rev and fade away between the ditches. I stood in the doorway and felt shaken up. The cat was watching me from under the fuchsia hedge, her body all pink now and reflecting the boiling sun as it sank in a pristine western sky. I went inside to find an old shilling on the table. He hadn't taken the plants. But I figured he had gotten what he had come for. Left me with something too.

*

It was several months later before I caught sight of this priest again. I'd heard, or rather overheard, that he'd not been well; had gone away for a while, hadn't been seen about. The winter had come on cold and dark and one wet Saturday evening I was in the village shop bartering for my weekly groceries — I'd bring in a box of vegetables to Oliver Nangle in the shop and try and swap them for tea and a few tins and some cold meat or whatever. This wasn't the easiest process, but the result was usually alright. Handy enough for onions and ordinary cabbage but understandably tricky when it came to my sparkier produce.

'Bok what?' Oliver grunted through teeth that clenched

a burning Players, the ash, as always, about to tip on the ham he was slicing or into the sugar he scooped into a bag.

'Choy. Bok Choy. It's like a tight little cabbage. Chinese.'

'Jesus, I don't know, Eamon. Chinese is it. Would anybody want it? There's talk of a Chinese restaurant coming to Trim. Be the hokey. Never heard the like. Bok Choy... huh?'

A couple of women had come into the shop on their way up to evening mass and mentioned that the priest was back.

'Oh, I much preferred when he was away. Sure that young Father Pat was only gorgeous. Oh, I'll miss him up there with his guitar and his big black curls.'

'Get away out of that, sure haven't you got big black curls of your own at home?'

'Yeh. Out in a field. Oh God, the PP is very dry though.'

'You can't beat the young priests now. I love the new folk masses.'

I decided to let Oliver off the hook on the Chinese cabbage. I had a better idea. I hadn't been next nor near a church for years, so it was just an impulse that took me. I'd recently been recalling to my brother the day Elvis died — the day of the priest's visit; so I was curious too. It would be interesting to see this jazzer in action on his own stage.

I skipped in under the torrents from the black thunderous sky and sat in at the back of the church just as the lacy procession of altar boys led out from the sacristy. I recognized his shuffle as he came out behind them, and I thought that the heavy vestments could crush him. He struggled through the ceremonies making only the odd faint sound. His sermon was inaudible and interrupted by his sickly coughing that resonated with the waxy smell from the wooden pews. I'd go on up to his house later and try and see him.

*

The housekeeper looked suspiciously at the little cabbages, but she took them and marched off to the kitchen, holding one in each hand like grenades that might go off if she didn't get them to the larder fast. I waited in the dark musty hall with the tocking of a grandfather clock for company. The parochial house was a big grim affair just outside the village. It had once been a glebe-house but now all of its better features, such as the window frames and gardens, had disappeared and had been replaced by something ugly and modern. The driveway had a plain feel with hedge-to-hedge tarmac and the hedges themselves were a uniform yellow laurel. The housekeeper showed me into a massive drawing room that had a dim fuggy green hue. There was a more homely corner that he had created for himself to one side of the big fireplace, in which a fire still sparked. He sat in a little armchair with cushions, a rug on his lap, and was lit from a standard lamp, with a tasseled shade, over his shoulder. A card table was laden with paper and a few books. I recognized the title on one. 'Ah yes,' he said, picking up on my curiosity, 'yes, I have been revisiting your beloved Russians. Frightening.'

As the dimness dissipated, I could see that the room was chock-a-block with a whole mishmash of furniture. It'd probably seen a thousand committee meetings. There was an old chaise-longue upholstered in a sort of greeny velveteen, several unmatched armchairs, various dining-room chairs, two big bookcases in the alcoves with diamond-panelled glass doors, a scattering of low tables and a piano. The floor had a nondescript dun carpet, covered here and there with very old and beautiful silk rugs. Who had had the taste for the silk? I sat on a large beige *à-la-mode* settee, with a faded cover. It was the dominating piece in the gloomy room.

'So, you've been away?'

He gave me one of his more petulant looks and told me that he had needed to take some time 'out' — that he wasn't back to full duties yet. Everything about him told me that here was a man going through his tortures. Tortures matched by the mouldiness of the green wallpaper, with its darker *fleur-de-lis* pattern, occasionally accentuated by a flash of lightning in the intense darkness pressing on the panes of the two large windows.

'Yes. So yes, have you ever had to question anything fundamental in your life? Ah well, you are very young. But still.' His voice was faltering, and he spoke even more deliberately and slowly than when we'd met previously. I allowed a silence and considered my next remark.

'I brought you your cabbage.'

Whereas before he'd looked washed out, I now thought as I looked at him, doll-like in his chair, that his yellowing delicate skin might be torn like old parchment and his bones crumbled to dust by a crack of the thunder.

'Atrocious.' I referred to the weather. He looked at me with a kind of curiosity, or fear — which, I couldn't be sure — chewing and sucking at his lips, his terrified eyes a question.

'I would like to play the piano for you. But I am no longer able.'

The fingers of his right hand flexed and gripped the arm of his chair. I could see, in the contortion of his features, the effort he made to conceal the quiver in his left hand; trying to steady those fingers, until he finally managed to grip with them too.

'Here, let me help you. I'm sure you can manage something. You would like that.'

I helped him over to the piano. I almost had to carry him, so unsteady were his steps, but the slightest of smiles threatened to crack open his face. He settled himself on the stool and managed to join his tremulous hands. I opened the sheet music on a Chopin nocturne. He studied the page and then looked up at me, somehow achieving a wryness in his expression.

'Be patient with me now.'

He managed the first few notes, falteringly like his voice, and then miraculously the melody began, like someone else had started to play. The fingers of his right hand moved with a strained fluidity across the keys while his left hand had somehow started to pick out a broken but matching rhythm. The piece he played — I can't remember which number — was even more complex and beautiful given the painstaking nature of his action. The slow cascade of the rich notes of the melody was powerful against the melancholic beat. It hit me in that cleft at the back of my neck. 'Bring on the night,' I thought, listening to this controlled rapture, watching this sick man melt into his playing. It hit me then that he might well be dying. Had something miraculous inveigled me as a witness to this, his last effort, his last plea, for the aesthetic? It completely blew me away.

A pale rent was showing in the black sky where it joined the low tree line to the west. The rain had stopped, and I moved impulsively to open a window. There was a thin sweetness to the harmonic of dripping water that penetrated from the outside with the current of cool air. I stalled for a while in that promise of Spring and nourishment. I turned, too late to seek permission, and saw that he had made his own way back to his dainty comfort by the fire, a puckish glint in his eye.

*

I never saw the poor man alive again after that night. Not long after, in the shop one day, I heard of his passing and made enquiries about the funeral arrangements. His name was Ivan Moore. I went back into that room in the parochial house to find the big beige settee had been replaced by trestles supporting his coffin. He was arranged in a brown habit. I felt those notes from the piano, like an opiate flow into me and I touched his sage-tinted, marble forehead to share this with him. I thought he might have thrown me one of his looks or tossed me back the jumping chords of Miles. He looked good, and wise, like he could be in a warm bed in Kansas City or San Francisco, with his own. In some peculiar way, this priest, this man, had managed to release me... give me something. Grace? No, gave me a bit of himself. Some martyr then. Both of us?

At the rainy graveside there were just a few of the older folk from about and only one stranger — a tanned elegant man, sharply dressed in a black overcoat, a pink paisley scarf, holding aloft a black umbrella and with a sprig of snowdrops in a neatly gloved hand. A dark tiredness stained his eyes and he continuously brushed wisps of lustrous white hair from over the thick, darker sideburns that cut into his deep-lined cheeks. There was a rhythm to his hand movement, and I tuned to it. It could have been Chopin or Davis, but I settled for a low humming — 'Heartbreak Hotel' — and I found that 'lonely' place with an ease of my own.

SAVIOURS

I. Fledglings

Up under the mother's blanket, beneath the tin roof, brother and sister watched the door for anyone who might return. There was nothing else in the room to make any sound.

'Do that thing ag'in, Danny. The thing with your lips.'

'Mammy says I shouldn't be at that. She says it'll bring me to the dark place sooner.'

'Not to mind the mammy. She'll be away in her own dark place now sure. Do it please. Make the noise.'

Danny fixed his lips, skint for all sorts of want, into the O-shape and pushed out the bassy vibrato that would excite his young sister. The little one made a weak shape of her own lips in imitation. She whispered in her awe.

'I don't know what it sounds like, but surely it's bether than the noises that the baests do make. You with your brain going on.'

'You have a brain inside you too, Mary-P. That's how you do your thinkin' sure.'

'Yeah, they say it's the brains that make us differ. Are we differ, Danny? Like who'd know if we were? All thim other brainy wans lookin' at each other only, is what I'm sayin'. Mebee it'd want a thing with more than brains to figure us out?'

'A thing with no brains at all, sis?'

'That's a thing. But how'd anythin' without brains be doin' any thinkin'? Have the thinkin'... or the knowin'?'

'That's the thing I'm sayin', sis. Only us wans with the brains, the human wans, can know what's goin' on with the other human wans.'

'I think you might be right. But how's it then about the mammy? And what was that last daddy thinkin'?'

'Goin' away like?'

'Yeah. Goin' off like that to wherever. How come he didn't know? How come the mammy didn't either? How you know... what'd become?'

'Become of us, sis?'

'Yeah, us. What's to become of us?'

'The priesh, he says we're to be saved. Do what unkie says, says he, and we'll be saved. What kinda savin' is that? Savin' from the unkie is what we need, sis. I'm not able to cut the throat of that unkie Molly fella, sis... couldn't even stick him. And all that stickin' he's after doin'. He's too thick. Everywhere. No sis, I think we'd be put away in a turf shed somewhere. Locked in.'

No one was ever sure when the mammy might come back. Sissy Molloy. Wasn't she coming and going all of her time. And down in the Buidéal. Sloppin'. A good bit beyond in the brother's too. Uncle Mikey-Dan Molloy. Unkie Molly. Stinkin' the place out with their faggin'.

*

One time, no one knew the hell where she'd got to. No sign about, and no word up from Cloch or over from the islands neither. And no one talking to the Guards for fear the little children might be put away. The unkie was in, and the tubby priest, saying she'll not be too long. Big Annie made them soup and got them to school on most days. The young slip of a teacher unable to raise a word either. And in the night-time there was unkie. Unkie with his pawin' and his thing. And the great fear of that thick bollocks. Too thick to cut.

'Here, do you think, Danny if... you know the mammy... say she was never, you know, to come back here. What'd that be like so for the you and me?'

'Well, she might never be back, sis. That's for sure. She could be off findin' a da. Gettin' to the bottom of that. At the dark end of somewhere.'

'Yeah, but what'd it be like for us if she... was... no more like? Do you not think, Danny, that they'd get us a new mammy? To look out for us and keep thim oul' miseries out of our... oh how'm I to say? Would the priesh go on with his savin' some place other? Would it stop the unkie doin' his tricks?'

'Well, that would be a worthit thing, sis. No more bleedin' out of our... sorry sis.... You may have your nub of it there, sis. But what then if the mammy she did come back? What then with more of her comin' and goin'? Sure it'd never end.'

'Well Danny, we need to think up a plan for doin' if she do come back then.'

'What kindofa plan you thinkin', sis? In your brain over there?'

'A plan that'd see us all right, and bring us a differin' kind of a savin' I'm thinkin'. I'm thinkin' someday we might cut an easier throat for all that. Thinner, Danny.'

*

Well, the mammy she did turn up. In the General Hospital above. Crawling about and mumbling her old nonsense. They called the priest and it was settled that she'd go up to The Mental and be all fixed up. That she may come back down then. And not a word to anyone who mightn't see it that way. Let them all stay away out of it. Sure the unkie and the priest would see to the little pair. And mild Annie in her filthy apron. And the skinny teacher wan. Sissy came back, and soon enough her coming and going started all over again. And so too the fumbling and the pain.

And sure times got a lot worse for Danny and Mary-P. They were growing and were mostly fed, but the unkie and the priest were slipping about them too, raining ruin. But they were indeed growing. Danny came up to the end of the primary, and he a little bullock of a lad who had kept his muscles strong 'with liftin' and runnin' and workin' on things' as he'd say. He could lift Mortimer's mangle above his head, but he kept that to himself so's to give his brain a chance to match up. That was Mary-P's notion.

'Danny you have the strength now for the deed, but like we was always sayin', it's the brainy bit that'll be the differ.'

'You have it right, Mary-P, but you know the next time she's gone... and then when she's back ag'in... that'll be the when of it there.'

*

Sissy Molloy looked like the skin of her could not have been drawn more tightly about her miserable bones. In her face she was a worn-out ninety when her papers said she was just over the thirty mark. Maybe those years were enough for her to suffer, and the end wasn't such a bad thing. Except in the manner of its coming. She had a sort of a looseness, easy to understand, to her habits that made advantage for others. Men really. If you could call them that, for most of them hadn't waited for their brains to catch up — or maybe with the way things were, they weren't allowed, by the powers-that-be like. And there was only the one power that was. And it holy and slithery. All these late-coming brains could cause a lot of havoc, and terrible absences too for the likes of a Sissy. Well, she couldn't be let grow a bigger brood, and weren't the unkie and priest in on the whole trick? Cod-o'-the-loop lads. But in or not, neither of them saw it coming. And on a holy day, when there were ceremonies for the most part, the opportunity arose. Sissy was on one of her home-times. Mostly in the cot, what with the bit of recovering she was needing. Danny and Mary-P were above in the other room.

'Now maybe we should have a prayer, Mary-P. Is there any oul' yoke you'd like to be aksin' for?'

'Well, there is the wan thing, brother. The way you are Danny, you know, and that's it.'

'Yeah, I'm the Danny you are mentionin'. So?'

'So how come you are Danny and I'm Mary... P?'

'I see where you're headin' to. Is it not... is it not that P was your daddy so?'

'Yeah, but who in the name of the Lord is P? And how come you have no P?'

'Well sis, you know I been thinkin' before about that. My idea is no one only she know who P is, and no one, not even she, know what in the name of Jaysus Christ lether to add to me. She dunno.'

'You mean P is my daddy and she dunno who your daddy is?'

'Yeah, she know P but she know no wan for me. That's the way of the mather.'

'Well holy be to whoever thim all is, that's no way to have us got.'

'That's another because-thing you know... on top of

all she's let pile in on us.'

'Danny, we need no more becauses. Let's do the brain thing.'

There wasn't a sharp thing involved in the end. Blades would be used later for sure, in a grown-up way. This pair were still only fledglings, still in a childhood. But they were caring about some brightness up ahead. Wary they were though. And it was easy to figure out that the mammy with her coughin' and splutterin' and her faggin' didn't have the best of chests, so what difference a bit more gasping and no air getting in. A job for the pillow. Her eyes so sunk. Like suns that went down so long ago they weren't worth looking into anymore, so where was the devil in it? There wasn't much gasping in the end anyway, and the eyes closed up quick, if they'd been ever open. Not a bit of a struggle, and she was free from her Ps and whatever. Choked by herself, they'd say. That was the way of it and damned if a soul got too worried.

Sissy was put down with her own people. The priest and the unkie got some fright though. They had the brains nearly 'catched-up' and they could do some figuring. Well, some working out, but they were feeling the fear too. And they had things to be afeared of surely. Danny was a strong boy and Mary-P had her brain. So better they be put into the care of the *powers* until... well until they might forget. Yes, Danny and Mary-P should be locked up for a bit. They surely then might let things be, if the burying was deep enough. Wasn't that the way the hurt went in? Into a deep place. Th'oul' shame concealed up in the thatch of their little brains. Like in all the other brains. Yes, that was the right contraption to get out of this. Just like you'd hide something bad in another's straw, so's it'd never be found in your own. Shame in a secret savings bank, to flash on rainy days. The terrible cuts from what the priest and the unkie'd been at with the little ones so well hidden, that those big bollocky boyos could go free as the birds. All of it a class of a mystery. And the powers-that-be were so fond of oul' mysteries, miseries and contraptions, that nothing would ever snake up — come back to bite no one. Well, that was the theory of it anyway.

So there was no new mammy. No one saw any use for that.

'Danny, do you think when we're grown bigger we might just forget about it all? Now that the unkie and the priesh might be laevin' us be?'

'How could I know what I'll remimber, or what will be in your brain, when we're a bit bigger? I know what I know now. That's all I know. I'm not sure what's to become of us in truth.'

'Best wait and see so, Danny, 'til we get bigger. That'd be the job.'

'That'd be the job awright, Mary-P. Only we might get a bit thicker too, into the bargain.'

II. Smoke

Danny didn't know how it happened that he woke up there. His last memory was of being in his own shack two miles over. He was slumped in the chair but he managed to shift a gaze upwards. A thread of smoke hovered like a kite over a mess of grey in an old hearth. Unkie Mikey-Dan's. A painful dryness soaked his muscles. He wanted to get up but something stopped him and said not to look behind him, not to move.

A nauseating lightness caused him to close his eyes. There wasn't a sound. The silence was long, and he may have lost a bit of consciousness as he struggled to remake time. After who knows how long, he heard a dog barking somewhere. Then a rising noise outside some place, someone coming, until he heard harsh scraping and a sound like a door squeaking. Something scur-

ried in the depths of the room. Then the dog stopped
its rumpus and there was more silence in which he remained alert. After a while a voice squealed.

'Brother, you must wake up now.'

Mary-P. But there was something else too.

'Oh Mikey-Dan. Mikey-Dan?' Danny wasn't a whisperer
but the dryness in his throat squeezed his voice now so
that it could barely be heard. He'd managed to get to his
feet and was looking across the room. A dusty stream
of light came from the small window beyond the door.
It reached the crumbling plaster on the back wall of the
bare room, extended in by the width of a few feet and
caught the head of the iron bed. It lit the awful pallor
of Mikey-Dan's face. The rest of his uncle's nude grey
shape was in shadow. Mary-P was standing at the far
side of the bed in the gloom. Danny guessed at the slith-
erer that he'd heard earlier astir. Stepping ever closer,
he reached out into the light at the forehead that seemed
to float. Expecting the warm moist feeling of putty, he
got a shock at the cold bony sensation. His uncle's eyes
were staring up at the tin roof and Danny recoiled at
the realisation that hit him.

'Gone. Since these ages. I was over to phone the
priesh.' He began to hear Mary-P's confused commentary.
His sister was always wittering away about something or
other and he had learned to shut it out so that her talk
mingled with the barren texture of the hills. Now somehow he tuned into it and her words were as loud as trum-
pets.

'The doctor will be aksed here by him.' She said it like it was the most mysterious thing in the world.

'What's after happenin'? How did this...? How long has he been there... like that?'

As he let the thoughts fly he was working his memory to get some picture, some recall, of what had gone on or where he had been — for what, for how long? Mary-P kept up her chatter, talking to herself, the rhythms and cadences of what she said ebbed to almost silence again as she got ready to send out another long and awful *ooooooh*. Her *Miserere*. Danny could tell, without hearing her words at all, just from the pitch of her little cries, that there was something more than sadness or grieving that was playing at her. Her tone had that steel-thread ring to it that spoke from the reliquaries of bad old deeds. What bad deed had we here?

'What bad deed, Mary-P? What has been done here... to this uncle, our friend, our cousin?'

'He were aksin' for it. Since I was a chile. Since we's chil'ern, you knew and ya wouldn't do anythin' then. About it like. But now ya done it. Ya done it good and right. Together we done it.'

'What was done together? Who did what together? What?'

'We done evertin' now together. Ha, would ya look at the thing on him now!'

Danny looked harder at the grey heap of his uncle. His eyes getting used to the landscape of it now — he could see clearly the winey, clotted gore at the man's groin. He gagged as he struggled to right his thinking.

'Oh Mary and Joseph sister, what's after goin' on?

Who diddled poor Mikey-Dan? Where's it flung to?'

Mary-P began an eerie wailing that doubled her and took her into the chair. Danny could hear she was laughing and he was relieved that they were still on earth. He began to move and stumbled, through his bodily constraints, over to where he could find her look. He shook himself out in front of her and grabbed her wide cheeks in his hands. Her greasy curls tangled in his fingers as he lifted her ruddy face, her eyes glistening in a rapture that he could not begin to understand. He asked her over and over what had been done; and though now he knew, he could see what was real in front of him, he still had no idea about the how.

'Aks the dog. The dog knows. Go on. Aks him what he done with it. Hee hee. The dog is the divil in this detail. Some detail too. He was some detail, our ol' unkie,' Mary-P squealed on.

Danny released her face, which dropped like she had no neck, and went for the door. And stopped. He turned again to the bed and the naked remains. His mind raced faster than the chant that was coming from the slouch of Mary-P before the hearth. He looked for a change, for some semblance of time rewinding into a *before* place, a better place to understand, to make better. But no. The fire was gone and the smoke had flown off too. There would be no healing in this stony, bare shambles of a room. Then he remembered what she had said. About the priest.

'Mary-P, you called the priesh you said? Did you get him? Will he be comin' now?'

'That buck too. That fella's be on his way. Oh yes,

that fella too. On his way. On his own way. Sure, now they did it together. They all did it. Together. Do you remember when I was in the river?'

'We bether cover him.'

Danny heard again the yelping of the dog. Scratching at the door. Scraping. He'd better be kept out. Put up with his whimpering. Deal with him later. Jesus he thought, he'd better go and check that animal out. Sure, if what Mary-P said... surely he'd seen it himself? Calm the dog. Clean the doggie. The puppy bether be cleaned up of his mouth before any petting priesh come by. Calm the Mary-P first. A smoke.

First he got her to stand by the bed with him. Mary-P picked up Mikey-Dan's grey underpants but they struggled to get them fully on him, lifting his legs gingerly as they were terrified of upsetting the wound for more bleeding. They found his torn pants and a sweat-stained jumper and managed to get them on him, in a fashion. It didn't look great but there was nothing else to use. Mary-P said she would take off her skirt but Danny said no, with the priest coming. They thought then they might get a sheet of roof iron that had fallen in on the outhouse but Danny threw his own greasy anorak over the lower bits and it neatened things up. After that, they kicked all the bottles and cans into a dark corner and that made the place look like an empty shed. Empty that is but for the life passed and the lives still going on. Danny found a candle in an old biscuit tin and he set it up on a crate he moved to the end of the bed. Mary-P pulled her lighter and a packet of fags from the band of her drawers and lit the candle and two smokes. She passed one across the body to Danny.

'Do you think it might be right to be smokin' up the room with the priesh comin'?' She asked as she exhaled her first drag into Mikey-Dan's staring eyes.

'It'll be awright.'

'Sure, don't they be always smokin' up the chapel around the dead craturs.'

'They do.'

'I don't think this lad is lookin' great at all.' She leaned in over the grey face again with a leer. 'I was sayin' to Danny that you're not lookin' too good now, unkie. Not at your besht today at all.' She laughed as she tipped her ash onto the cover above his groin.

'Mind out now. We don't want to set the whole place goin' up.'

'Sure there's nothing in here to burn.'

'There's us, isn't there?'

'Sure a burnin' is what's in it for us. Soon enough.'

'Is that what you're thinkin' so?'

'Amn't I after sayin' it? Soon enough. Oh yeh soon enough. The lad with the big poker for us.'

'Still, we might get to go up to the other place.'

'Up in smoke. Poker up me curly arse.'

They smoked on in muttering silence around the dingy catafalque until they could barely see each other; worker wraiths hanging around waiting for their final orders. Mary-P's chatter rose in the fog.

'Thim prieshs have no women of their own eeder.'

*

In fairness, Mary-P had quietened down a bit by the time Moloughney, the priest, came in, although she was beside herself when they heard the car pull up and the dog howling. Danny had forgotten to clean up the hound and put it in a shed. He would go for the weak man — particularly an unshaven man in a collar. Molougney had steadied the dog by stopping dead himself and drawing himself up as The Almighty Man's man, followed by a little grab of the growler's jaws. There was a smear of blood on his own paw after that. He had felt it as dog dribble.

The decrepit old priest of a thing moved about tremulously in the haze, making the best of blessing Mikey-Dan and sealing him with the holy fluids (mingled now with a little blood from his petting of the dog). He daubed from the small silver cylinders he fetched with stubby blood-stained fingers from his greasy trouser folds. Danny hoped that Mary-P's lips would stay sealed too. But this priest had a sibilance (that may have been the result of ill-fitting teeth or it might have been simply a lazy slur) and Mary-P had a way of imitating what she regarded as high and mighty. She didn't quite take the mickey, as that would have needed a higher knowing on her part but she could come dangerously close. As the priest intoned over the corpse, Mary-P intoned from memory.

'Lesh ush lift up our hearts and give thanksh and pray... for He hash taken away the shins of the world...'

The priest and Danny both threw dirty glances at her as her pitch rose. Danny had been happy that they were nearly there with this end of the business and didn't want any disturbance of that fact. Moloughney, in his attempt at damping her, opened his eyes wide but instead of his disapproval only managed to show his eyes as the bloodshot querulous jellies that they were and prove he was actually a little drunk. In fact, he did manage to quieten her by accident for, as he took his eyes off his work, his thumb crossed Mikey-Dan's lips in a way that made them quiver. At the sight of this, Mary-P's mouth fell open as she thought Moloughney had somehow revived something in Mikey-Dan.

'Ooooh, his lips just moved. Is there a breath yet in him?'

This startled Danny who had been trying to stare Mary-P into quietening down. He darted a look at the head of the corpse but he saw the lips were frozen closed again and the eyes still stared out from the yellowing greyness. The priest had reined himself in too and was wrapping up his sacramental duties. He took the purple stole from his neck and fumbled it into his pocket. As he did, he dropped one of the little silver cylinders and it hit the boards and rolled away into the gloomy corner. Danny went down behind it and followed the roll of it into a large hole in the boards. It shimmered from sight.

'Shaints alive, it ish gone from shight.' The priest looked for a reaction from Danny.

'Under the boards.' Danny had no more intention than the other two of putting his hand down into that rat-hole.

'Leave it sho. The Guards can fesch it. They'll have to come, you know. And the doctor. Shee'sh the only one who can shay how hee'sh dead.' Moloughney chewed out his words as he made for the door, throwing hopeless glances at everything in the room.

*

Death by murder in that rocky valley, where crows perch on the parched skeletons of dead sheep, is not as uncommon as you might think. Human lives have been shrunk and dropped on the spot in these parts for centuries. The dessication of the bones scattered and clawed at around Mikey-Dan's pitiful door follows in a line from the scarification of his ancestors' bones by starvation.

Butchering is a life-skill and Danny had known sharp instruments: knives, saws and hatchets. Cold in his hand, he understood the keenness of blades and could direct a cutting edge to any end. He knew too the clammy sweat of pill-dazed hours and the confusion of walls and fences, where nothing ever began and nothing ever ended. How you could be somewhere and go away and then come back and never remember. Never understand the desolation of words spoken from the sick pit of a hungry stomach; forget all thoughts that swam in the dreams of neat alcohol — his mind like an autumn leaf shaking in a light whiskey breeze. Whatever understanding existed, it was scented by the stench of his body, leaking through the worn threads of his poverty and seeping down into his heavy boots — his only stability.

Oh yes, they could come at you from behind, left or right. They could come with stones or fists like stones. They could come too with the heavy thread of official tyres or the shocking imprint of the harp (an instrument not tuned lightly by those who came for him). But he was used to that. All his head could ever hold were the numb images and ringing words of his condemners. In his narrow-skulled, hard-boned, taut-skinned, smelly-haired head. A head that no one cared for. It would end up inside in a bottle or under a rock. Split and bled out, shrunken or crushed. Parched. Oh yes, his own rubber would harden and crack and he'd be well rid of the cramping skin too and sure the birds would mind his bones. Join their spirit to the soul-thing they talked about. Mind him. That left him to deal with the one, the clearest image of them all — the bloody meat of the heart. Its shape was the most normal thing he could think about. Its place the most obvious of all, hidden and minded there, where his own mother's had been for him.

*

The Guard placed the silver cylinder in Moloughney's palm. He didn't press it as he felt it might need another wipe — they had been afraid to wash it but had rubbed the worst of the gore off it.

'You wouldn't have liked to have seen what we found there under those boards. Hopefully there's an end to it soon.'

The priest blinked out from swollen eyes. The figure before him a wrack of blue serge. He wondered blankly what was the fuss.

*

Doctor Sheelagh O'Flaherty put her phone on silent and laid it down on the book of poetry that lay open in her tweed lap. She was composing her reply. The Guard she had just spoken to had thanked her for her help up at Mikey-Dan Molloy's and told her that she would be asked as a witness in the case against the niece and nephew. She put the phone back off silent and gave her answer.

'There'll be no need for that. I'm only a witness to what was rightly coming. There should be no judge nor jury here except ourselves and all that we should have said and done before. That old fella got his due. Those poor, poor children and the rape he brought. If only we had the words and the way to have dealt with it all. And as for the holy man himself. The less said. No. No evidence against those poor souls from me.'

She left the Guard off to his duties politely and for now she would take comfort in her solitude with Mozart's 'Requiem'.

*

Danny lifted his tobacco pouch and stubbed into it for a roll. A tense jig fluttered from the transistor on the slimy formica table. The batteries were about to go. He hated the Guards and their smell of soap and god knows what. Blown up boys. Surely no good could be coming. If there was a thing at all he could grasp hold of and understand in all the palaver.

*

The broken seat of the lock-up toilet lay half beneath Mary-P in the narrow space between the bowl and the wall — her arms wrapped around it. The suffocation of her lungs was smeared about her; puke and blood mingled with her piss and shit. Her fag burned out.

Earlier, Mary-P had seen a little flicker of panic in Danny's stony eyes, a little darkening was all. It gave her a kind of a knowing, an impulse for the little that was left.

*

The voice of the judge was accented, different than the voices of the hills and had a sureness that set it apart.

'... clear that the motive here was beyond the normal... nothing tangible to gain... no property to speak of... no land or material goods... or any inheritance at all. Here we have one of the poorest in this land dispatched from life in a heinous manner by a dog who might have been richer than himself. A terrible tragedy with no discernible motive whatsoever...'

That powerful man had sung away his concerns by the time his car had finished its journey back east that evening.

*

'We pray for thee, sweet child of Eden, Mary-P. You are a safe wan now.' Danny was talking fast as he said good-bye to his sister in the hospital, where they would fix her broken little soul. 'They are going to look after you here and mind you for a little while. We are free. And I'll do my own long time one way or the other. A piece of time back for me. And sure, we'll take all 'em tablets too. Oh gawd, that unkie, he was a terrible hawker, a terrible piece. And you, you little mite in your summery yellow dress and sandals. Your curls and your flowery blue eyes. Oh, you were a sight. And the monster he... he... oh the bollocky monster. Well, you did for his diddle. He'll play no more on that. Did and done it proper. The dog jumped over the moon, Mary-P. Hey diddle-diddle... hahaha... and the rat ran away with his tune... Here, we'll have a smoke to that sure.'

III. Saviours

It was black. Black as the ribbons festooned on Motor-man's door after they had done for him. Some sort of a hood, tight at his neck, and if indeed his eyes were open, they had filled with the black, the essence of dark. Flooded with blood like his ears? His whole body felt like it had been shredded. The tracks of the shot-gun pellets throbbed and then seared like embers fanned in a fiery rhythm. Why had they not done it to the head? Karine's howling? But sure he was never meant to be found. Was this con-sciousness or something else? What did exist was a cold bouncing metal floor and these thoughts somewhere. And the sensation of rivets.

*

The headlights danced a crazy pattern on Mary-P's Sacred Heart. Like in the lightning, but longer. Filtered by the evergreens. Like the moon, they sharpened Jesus's soft eyes and russet heart — the bitter thorns holding their grip. She was up and fingering the corner of the net curtain to see. The engine noise came up faint from the bog. The lights steadied and then popped off. There was silence again.

*

The scrape of a metal hinge and a draught of cool air confirmed in him some sort of awakening. Then there was an urgency of voices and manhandling, until it all went away again and he was just a heap on wet ground. Then the dizzy spin and the sickening drop. The voices came once more and began to fade as a weight of something increased on him. He was inside the sodden earth.

*

Mary-P, in her coat, stood in the tree-line and watched the two figures below finish up their digging. It was raining. They rolled the bundle into the bog-hole and filled it back, clodding it up with clumps and sods. Then they heaped it with rocks. They pissed on the tomb and then loaded up, turned carefully and drove away to oblivion.

*

'There was some class of a kick or a twitch. I don't know to be honest how I saw it but I kinda knew the fella wasn't gone, dead, you know.'

'You've the eyes of an oul' hawk. D'you know that, Mary-P? An' a doe's ears into the bargain. Little escapes you.'

'G'way out of it, Danny you. Sure there's no one believes me an' a thing I see. Didn't that priesh exa-communicate me nearly when I told him about unkie Mikey-Dan an' the killin' palaver over, the years gone?'

'An' that feckin' sergeant a kinda hintin' at the wrong lockin' up? You are bether off away out of it. With your own door for your own lockin'. All of us I say. Here tell us what's goin' to happen so with the near-corpse fella? He won't be healin' up easy after all that bleedin'.'

Still alive, he was stretched on the settle under a warm blanket, just outside the glow of the fire but close enough to let the warm currents help his thaw. They had doused him with a stinging white spirit and tried to staunch the bleeding with strips of clean sheets. Mary-P had mopped his fever and given him sips of warm milk, like she would a kitten. *They had reassured him and calmed him so that he had stopped struggling to remember the digging-out and the carrying to this warm place and all that had happened before. He was in and out of sleep and consciousness and their words only came in snatches that made little sense, but their talk was nonetheless of great comfort. The very fact that he could hear their voices kept him going.*

*

Mary-P was over at the ramshackle sink, scraping something out of an old pot while Danny paced up and down
behind her. She was wondering.

'For sure, it's all worth thinkin' about for a bit.
There could be a followin'-on from all of this.'

'Bether we just call for the doc so?'

'Could be. But could also be that the fella here
needs not knowin' if you get my drift. He could be one
o' thim... you knows... under the radioar min. An' thim
other lads, who plugged him, sure they might get the
tip-off agin.'

'You are thinkin' correct, Mary-P. Lordy knows but
it's ourselves they'd think done the horror. Didn't they
the one time afore, as you say, over the unkie. Mebee
we'd have a been bether off to laeve him in his drownin'.'

'What do ya mean? Laeve him in his drownin'? How's
he been drownin'?'

'That's what woulda be happenin' in the bog-water.
Goin' in through his mouth an' his nose an' his eyes
who knows how else. Get him so he couldn't braethe no
more.'

'Drownin' in blood more like. Sure how'd he be braethin' anyway an' him all flaked up with the blood an'
all? He was dead o' bleedin' if we didn't come for him.
If your mad haevin' an' liftin' hadn't dragged him safe.'

'Well, if any o' thim slug-shots gets him inficted he won't be long braethin'.'

'Here, do you remimber that ol' ewe — the one that went nasty an' you got in a timper — that you blasted with pellets and we got her over it? Could we be savin' this fella oursels? Put an end to handin' him over an' blamin'. Laeve him off whichever way he wants to go.'

They stripped him bare and lifted him onto the table nearer the fire. The beads of carmine and sweat kept coming and flickering as they washed him clean over and over. He breathed like he was weeping — like he was in and out of being there. Danny cleaned a pen-knife in the white spirits and used it to pick out shot-gun pellets from the surfaces of the wounds and then he heated it to a blasted red in the fire to go deeper. The man rose to scream at the touch of the burning blade and then passed out entirely. Finally, they had done all they could and stood quietly, looking for the first time at the wholeness of him: the repose of his near-saved turf-black body, breathing heavy but more peacefully now. Jesus looked down, his eyes even softer and browner and his thorn-girdled heart reddening in the dawn light.

'Mercy me, I had him all coloured by the bog, Mary-P. Thought that after the washin'... but oh no this fella, he's a —'

'He's black, Danny. An' on my Aunt Annie, we've been savin' him so.'

*

Putting a day in around the place was easy as nothing
much ever changed and the chores were handy: cats and
chickens to feed, sweeping out, turf for the fire, pots
to scrape, kettles to boil. Once a week, Danny would
set off for the village, walking the distance to the
main road and hitching on from there with whichever
local or stranger thought to stop. It was a day's worth
of time. He would collect the social welfare for them
both — Mary-P being deemed an invalid — and come
back with a sack of shopping. Once a month he would
add the trek to the 'doc' — a severe but kindly woman in
tweeds who was their protector. Other than that, one day
followed the other in a mostly even flow with little to
upset or to excite — once the pills were all taken.

*

Big and all as the man was, Danny was that bit bigger
and they dressed him up on the second day in Danny's
yellowing shirt. They had burned his own destroyed
shirt and had washed his grey trousers (not before they
had both, separately and slyly, checked the empty pockets). A better bed had been made up in the settle and
they continued with washing and dressing the wounds.
The fever seemed to be quietening down and that gave
them some confidence but they watched carefully as the

man slept, their huddled shapes shadows in the evening as they whispered at the fire, the whites of their
eyes to be seen occasionally as they checked on him.
A great and wondrous dilemma had taken over their
existence.

'An' what are we goin' to do, so? An' even if the doc
did come, how'd ya think she could be keepin' it to hersel?'

'But the fella don't want to be left here. I think he
nodded that.'

'You dunno what's he noddin' at an' you proddin'
an' aksin' him all thim questions. We have to wait until
he's proper awake an' his mind thinkin' ag'in. I'd say
he's on the mend though.'

'There'd be the fear in him of thim other lads comin' ag'in. Thim shootin' lads.'

'We put that buryin' place back the same. We done
that. Sure how would they have the idea that he's not
still down in it. Anyways, they'd be afeared o' checkin'.'

'Yah. An' I pissed on it empty too. I did. Yah.'

There hadn't been a geeks of Church in the house, or a
normal prayer had never been spoken there, since the
day that their uncle Mikey-Dan was laid out and the fat
little priest had pressed them to 'confess' their crime to
the Lord God. That time, in the end, there was no proof
nor blame on them and the mad dog took the rap. Either
way the world had been ridden of a most heinous man—
one man down—but others were left and they both
knew this and harboured it. They knew what had gone
on with men before too and what Jesus had seen. That's

why he was left in his frame — a witness who would come down one day to tell it all, and end it all. They made their own prayers.

*

The third day with the saved-man came up slow and very rough. Outside, the pine trees bent madly and the branches of the ashes — their gorged roots secure hinges in the stony ditches — were one more time stretched horizontal. Storms were commonplace in the shorter days and it added to the anxieties from the darkness and the fragility of their shelter. The hens scattered and cats sneaked through every door. A pot went tumbling and Mary-P's pale knickers were torn from the line. She scurried about in her Wellington boots chasing hens in and cats out, and all the time her own scrawny paw held down her greasy skirt in defiance of the tumult. Stronger gusts tore down from the high bens scraping and rattling in the iron roof. The man woke into this unease as the pair now battened down in the room. *The air felt faintly sick and vacuous but he could risk a movement to test the pain. It didn't take a lot until he was corseted by the agony again, but he held it and held it until there was some equilibrium and he could breathe.*

'Holy mother of the divine, Mary-P, the fella's starin' up direct at the ceilin' an' the eyes of him are like the two bouls of hell. Come quick over an' have a peep.'

'I'm comin'. That stormin' will be addlin' him. Has he a word?'

He could see them come from the mullering brightness over and make them out. A wild-headed woman in a dirty pink cardigan and a burly man in a string vest and blue jeans. The man's hair was a toss of curly-red and, as his face came in closer, he saw that he had a girl's features and his two eyes didn't match. He tried to open his mouth and say something and it was hard, but he broke the gum seal on his lips and said his name.

'Is he after cursin' or what? Has he used the Lord's name?' Danny was flailing, his hands disturbed by this new pattern in affairs. 'Mister. Hey fella, what you sayin' there?'

'Sssh, calm it down. He don't look too great. I'd say he's afeared. Don't be afeared fella... we are savin' you.'

He could tell from their looks the kind of disturbed mood they brought, but he knew from the scatter of memory and the soaking warmth he was lying in that care was being given. The gale outside was now at its ferocious best and it upset the currents in the room. *He tried to smile but it came across as a growl of pain and it startled them. The man with the red hair reared back as if he was looking to find something to lift. The woman's mouth opened and he saw the stumps of her few black teeth. Their eyes were narrow and flickering and he could see they were frightened. He wondered how he was to keep the calm and he wondered too about the state of his ripped body. He moved a hand to his groin and felt the stickiness. It sent another ripple of pain through him. He lifted the hand and saw them rear back again, this time the man grabbing something and lifting it.*

Danny held back with the axe. All three of them were looking at the gory red hand that flashed in the light that came in with the storm.

'Hush it ag'in, Danny, can't you? This fella's not long for the road. Will you look at all that bleedin' ag'in.'

The main storm had passed and the darkness had settled in heavily. Rain still hammered the tin above them and the dripping had begun. The man had made several attempts to say something but even with *his greatest effort they appeared not to understand*. He had exhausted himself and interrupted any healing.

'You have the nose for that awright, Mary-P. This fella can't lasht here.'

'An' him not havin' the language a bit. Lord, thim were the strangest words I ever did hear. Like thim incanotations that the Quare Fella is said... there's more than the darkness nor his skin.'

'Well, it's the doc or nothin' now. We're done with this fixin' an' savin'.'

'Well, we be headin' for the blamin' an' the lockin' up so, Danny.'

'Sure we done nothin'. Wasn't he in the grave. Dead a bit.'

'Dead sure. Dead. You can only be dead the once.'

'What are you sayin', Mary-P? Dead the once?'

'Yah. Yah. That is it. Unless you're Our Saviour over.'

'Heh. Heh-heh-heh. Yah, we could wait but for how long could we be waitin'? He could be found afore he's dead ag'in. An' dead he'll surely be. Sure who in God's world can be waitin' or lookin' on the soul that's surely dyin'? The blaster or the skinnin' blade? Heh. Yah, we're done now with the fixin' an' savin' awright. It's the shootin' an' the buryin' ag'in now.'

*

There are heaps of rocks in the bogs and all over the valleys in those mountains. There are bones and there is quickening. Somewhere, always, in all the magnificence, there will be something short of knowing. But there is knowing and not knowing and who's to say which is the better sometimes? There is the walk to the end of the endless road. And then there is some bit of coming back. There are bones. There is quickening. There is saving and being saved. There are prayers and there are stories. And there are some things that are always pissed on.

BADLANDS

A skinny man with long dreadlocks dozed on a bog in the west of Ireland, his black skin warmed by a late autumn sun. He was interrupted by the sound of an engine, followed by the distant clatter of scraping and grinding metal.

'Irish John' Prentice had been happy to be away from Sheffield, removed from his birthplace, his songs and guitars, finding space. He'd sought his flown mother's people out — trying to get to grips with her O'Malleys. It was good cover for what he was really looking for: some spark to light up his head again. And the light was good — might be good enough to beam him back to the City of Steel. There were loads of O'Malleys but they weren't for much talking and there was no recall of his mother. Not a surprise, as names slipped easily from mothers of mothers. And some sort of an O'Malley she may well be, from somewhere else. He was happy to let her go. It was not really why he was here. Either way, the place had put on its blank face, however well it was lit: nothing to see here but yourself.

About ten miles into the mountains he'd thrown himself and his bicycle onto the heather. He'd been thinking of the pirate queen they'd told him about: Grace O'Malley. Could he put her to music he wondered. *Gracie*? *Gracie meets Calypso*? Ska? Nah. He smiled at the idea. There had of course been a fucking hymn to soften his head, a Stabat Mater — an echo of a concert he'd been at in an abbey a few nights previously. That had rightly cheered him up. So, he wondered, with all this good humour, maybe he was ready to go home.

He shifted himself to the top of the bank to see down the fifty yards or so to the twisty tar. There it was, a heap of metal, wheels up and still turning, smoking he thought. A goldy-brown blur of an animal rolled out of sight over a hillock beyond the ditch. 'Bugger this.' He set off, hopping the dry hummocks among the sphagnum, feeling the spiky grass against his bare feet. He clambered over a sheep fence and arched a path across the road, never taking his eyes off the inverted red car and a grey horsebox, now detached and thrown on its side. The windows of the car were dipping in the ditch water like they were on a sinking ship. He stooped in to look. There was straw hanging behind the glass. Hair. Rusty straw-coloured hair. Blood.

A heap of metal, a machine flung down, half-drowned in a drain, was a regular feature in that valley, but Prentice had never seen anything like this before.

The bog sucking hard on the terrible iron blew off any remnants of his reveries. He had shaped iron once, back in Sheffield. A foundryman. Before he had swapped those scars for the callouses from steel guitar strings. Now, in this wild and eerie place, the name of a lad from Rotherham came to his lips: Wilson, whose head he had seen crushed by an axle falling from a faulty gantry crane. He'd buried that image a long time ago.

He looked for a way to get the car open, but the doors and windows were jammed tight. His feet were sinking so he splashed back to firm sod. Some seconds passed before he sensed a volume of air being displaced behind him. A huge shadow caused him to stiffen. He turned to see a massive black hole with the outline of... a what... a cowboy? He fancied that something might be about to fly out from this shape. A silence settled in. Nothing moved in the vast emptiness stretching to the feet of mountains all around. Then suddenly a breeze stirred the grasses. A sound built into a shrill moan, then became a voice.

'Gone to fucking heaven.' This was from a garrulous world.

Prentice knew that he didn't need to say anything just yet. He tried to line his thoughts up, so he might find some words that could be driven in, like rivets, when he was ready.

'Gone to fucking heaven.'

A huge man came into the light, repeating his words. He rambled in on the Cuban heels of his snake-skin boots; under a white ten-gallon hat; a sky-blue suit flurried about his frame in the breeze. The diamante decoration — the ruby stones on the jacket, the silver studs on the trouser seams and the brown crochet patterns stitched on the shirt — made for a vivid pathos. He hitched his thumbs either side of the large horseshoe buckle of his belt to steady himself.

'I'm Shane. O'Malley. Shayneen O'Malley. Who'm I with here? What y'all go by, pardner?'

'I'm John. I'm English. My mother was from here. They call me Irish John.'

'Do they indeed. Can't see why.'

Prentice figured there was no use in fucking about with irony so he settled for the straightforward.

'My father was from Jamaica but there was English John and Scots...' He let his words trail off. The woman in the car was reclaiming his full attention. 'We need to get her out. Although it looks like she's—'

'Passed on to the angels,' O'Malley gurned out. 'Where's the damn hoss gone is what I want to know. Clear kicked his way out of that box. Bastard Palomino. Twisted... what's them things... genes. Yeah, them things. Never trusted that hoss. A bit like yourself, hah? You look like a fella with a bit of a twist in you. English did you say? From the colour of you I'd be thinking you are not at all. Or an Irishman for that matter. The most of you anyways. Did ya see a hoss? A Palomino bastard?'

A new arrival, a cloud, moved in to block the setting sun. In the cold shallow light they took one another in again: the dreadlocked, barefoot young Englishman and the ruddy-faced man with fine threads of orange hair squeezed out from under the rim of his hat.

'I didn't see a horse,' Prentice lied, 'but this here's not good. Are we going to try and get her out of there or... are you alright? You look as if...'

'As if what... what? That sure is a shock of a thing here... and the little child...' was the reply and then another question, 'are y'all an Apache or what?'

Prentice felt the sting of the words. 'What do you mean child? What child? What are you saying?' he heard himself ask. 'What Apache?' he thought, a burning in his head. 'What are you saying?' he asked again.

'Let's see what we got here.' O'Malley pushed roughly by and on into the ditch.

Both men were now peering in at a young woman's face, inverted, in a grotesque press against the car window. Still as marble. Her gaze was locked on some thought that no longer existed, and a trickle of blood came down from the gape of a mouth to implicate the eyes. Too late. There was no way to shift the doors and the car was slowly sinking. The men twisted their necks to see better, but nothing got any better. The dammed-up water in the drain was slowly reaching in to sink the terror. Prentice felt some unwanted words might drop out if he didn't right himself. O'Malley might have come upright for other reasons: fumes of alcohol were mingling with the evaporation of the motor fuel that was painting the boggy ditch water.

'Is that your truck?' Prentice caught the glint off bright metal from a dip in the road beneath the waning sun — the direction he guessed O'Malley had come from.

O'Malley was now bent forward, his massive body leaning down on his thighs, with the ten-gallon held across his knees. He let out a long sigh, nodded and then started to shake his head. The top of his head was tonsured and a long pelmet of fine orange hair shook across his features. Here was something brutal, Prentice thought. The breeze moved the flamy heads of the grasses all around.

'Were you ever with another man's wife?' O'Malley barked.

Prentice was getting used to the noise of the man — how the accent slipped in and out. But now he was making some new sound; it started like a buzz. O'Malley was humming something. Then he was singing. Prentice thought he recognized a few words and a tune he was familiar with. It was a song he'd known from Hank Williams, 'Your Cheatin' Heart'. It'd been played in a bar the night he'd arrived in the west. Now the way O'Malley chewed and spat the words it was hard to make out, but there was a sinister tone to it. 'Excuse me?' Prentice was well off-balance and frightened: the question and the venom of the singing.

'I said. Were. You. Ever. With. Another. Man's. Wife. Are you not hearing me? I said—'

'I heard you. What—?'

'You may well ask. Will you not listen to my question? Huh?'

'I'm sorry, mister, but I've no idea why you are asking me that. What's this about?'

'Fuck you, Turkishman,' rumbled O'Malley and then the nasty singing started again.

'My mother was an O'Malley... she...' Prentice fought with the need to start spinning out.

'There won't be much dancin' out of her again.' O'Malley made a clucking sound that Prentice heard as a low chuckle.

'My mother? She was—' Prentice tried to get something off the mark again.

'Your mother? What're you saying about your mother? How the hell is your mother in this? I'm talkin' about her here. Darleen.'

'How did she come off the road?' Prentice went to change the tempo again.

'I guess she needed to stop. Stop, do you hear?' Then again with the low chuckle—'Oh, she was stopped alright. In her tracks she was stopped.' Then he raised his voice. 'But I'm thankin' it's none of yer fuckin' business now, is it?' O'Malley was looking in several directions at once now, with his wavering blather. It was unclear what he was trying to focus on.

Prentice had moved back to have another look to see if there was any sign of a child. Of any life. Of a way in.

'I suppose I might try and drag this out with my rig.' O'Malley stumbled around to head off back to his truck.

'Hold on. Hold it up. For a minute, will you?' Prentice called loudly after him. 'We could do more harm. I can't see any child. Are you sure you saw a child?'

O'Malley stopped and turned.

'Jesus. I thought... What am I after sayin' about keepin' your nose...' he growled.

'You ran that woman off the road?'

'What're y'all sayin, huh? Did you say something about your mother? An O'Malley? That I... what did you say, I didn't... something? All I say is we'd better get that automobile out before it sinks altogether and drowns 'em into the bargain. We better get that automobile the fuck out of there. Do you hear, Geronimo? We can't let 'em drown too.'

There was a different temper now in O'Malley's tone as he waltzed back into his cowboy speak. He'd come back towards Prentice sure-foot, stretched out his arms, laid them firmly on Prentice's shoulders and gave him a bloodshot stare. The whiskey smell was powerful and Prentice saw the muddle in the man's eyes; his puckered childish face. He looked like he could be sixty or only a boy, a big boy. A big mad dangerous man-boy, Prentice figured, and he spoke to dispel the thought.

'The woman looks like she's dead and there's no sign of a child. Can we smash the glass?'

'Reinforced. And there'll be a child alright. Believe me there'll be a child. We'll drag it out.'

'But—'

'No, Injun-boy. I knows that woman. Darleen. Thar'll be a child.'

What abominable intimacy had he stumbled upon? This Irish... cowboy? He thought of looking for help— on his cycle in he hadn't noticed any house for a few miles back; he carried no phone and anyway wouldn't O'Malley...?

'Mister O'Malley. You from around here?' he shouted as O'Malley disappeared into the sinking light on his way back to his truck. O'Malley threw an arm up from his shambling departure.

The silver shimmering hulk came roaring up from the dip. The figurehead steer-horns on the fenders seemed to come straight at him and as it rose, so Prentice swung out of the way and into the deep skid ruts from the crashed car. O'Malley pulled up the massive silver truck and leaned out the window to answer Prentice.

'Yeah, I'm from around here. And I'm at thangs the way of 'round here.'

'We should call someone. An ambulance. Have you got a phone?'

'We'll call no one. This here's no one's business.'

'Isn't there a danger...?'

'The only danger for you is that you end up in there alongside the —'

'I just thought...'

'What did I just say? Eh, Injun?' O'Malley then picked up his song again — more about a cheatin' heart, and paying for it. He was out of the cab and lifting a coil of heavy rope from the bed of the truck. At the end of the valley, the sun came out of the cloud to bobble over a mountain and out of the day. Prentice felt a jolt as the huge gaudy figure brushed into him and shambled towards the car. O'Malley kept crooning away, louder now, to all the world like a satisfied man going about his work. And adamant about the price for cheating.

We're done here with this *Injun Geronimo* bollocks, Prentice thought and then he said it.

'Is there some problem with being black? Anyway, I'm not an Indian. Never was. I told you my father was from Jamaica. Me, I'm as English as Jack Charlton. That's what I am. My mother was Irish. That's why they call me Irish John.' He was both angry and afraid, so he tried to sound courageous.

'Y'all tell me your mother was from where? 'Round here? Pretty yarn. Jeez. It's all O'Malleys hereabouts. Pirates. You tell me y'all are an Englishman? Some sooty Englishman though.' O'Malley gave what might have been a soft laugh as he said it and went about lashing the rope over the car — he was preparing to right it with a sideways turn. 'An' you know pardner, I guess there could be a problem, and you with the tint an' all. It's not a thing an O'Malley mammy would be totin' hereabouts. But I'm just shapin' to deal with this here problem for now. Could be that I know that woman, your mammy. Could be I don't. And now if y'all don't mind.'

Prentice went back to check the woman. The light was greying fast and a soft rain was drizzling from thickening clouds. Water the colour of rust was seeping into the car and he couldn't see any face: the head had turned and settled in some other way. The blonde hair was now shivering like a water-weed. A pink Stetson hat floated like a jellyfish. He looked up to see that O'Malley had backed the truck up to get an angle for the pull. O'Malley was about to tie the rope to the hitch of the truck when he straightened up and turned, still holding the rope in a loop. His expression relaxed. The rain made a rapid plipping sound on his hat. The palm of his free hand shot up to rub his head, tilting the hat back at an angle.

'Tell me this', he said, with no sign of the earlier barrack in his voice. 'Do you know any of them supermodels? Over there. The supermodel ones?'

'I don't.' Prentice had been watching the car again. The air was cold, the rain was coming heavier and a loud gurgling noise from the car had come and gone before he heard the absurd question.

'Sundance. Flaherty. Said he poked one over at Ballyna-the-fuck-Castle, summer just gone. You don't happen to know Sundance, do you? Nah, I didn't think so. He's the boy for the cow-pokin'. Poke a steer too, the same bucko. Hah. It's anythin' with a sweet ass around here.' He made a sound like laughter again but there was no laughter in his voice this time. He came towards Prentice and placed the loop of rope over his head to rest on his shoulders. 'You look like a fella who'd know about pokin'. Did you say you were a pop-star boy or somethin'?'

Both men stared at the other. Teeming rain ran down Prentice's face misting up his vision. He struggled to figure out if the fright he felt was in the other man's eyes too.

'I didn't say. No, I'm not a popstar. I'm just a...' Prentice held it at that. He wished he held the five-pound hammer that he thought he'd never hold again. He imagined he did and stayed his ground.

'Huh. You're just a fella looking for his mammy. Or her mammy's mammy. You weren't going with any other mammys here, were you?' O'Malley opened the loop and pulled the rope sharply away across the back of Prentice's neck. It chafed sorely. 'There's a lot of mammys need laevin' be in this place. Don't need little strangermen pokin' about. Mixin' things up. That's when the rumblin' starts. If you get my drift?'

O'Malley then moved quickly, the rain flinging from the rim of his hat. His suit was drenched now and sticking to his frame like a tissue. A blue skin that was silver-studded to him. He fixed the rope to the hitch, swung up into the driver's seat and started the truck. He shouted over the engine noise at Prentice.

'Watch that mammy bitch come up. And her little man. And don't even think about the whys or the whats of it. Bad-assed mammys get what's a-comin to 'em. And their little babbies. Honeybunch here was a bad girl. And if I was you, I'd be a quiet boy... we'll get around to...' The revving of the truck drowned out the rest.

Prentice watched as the engine roared and the rope strained. The tyres on the truck slipped and screeched and sprayed until there was movement from the ditch. Then everything was moving and splashing as the crashed car was righted after a great sucking struggle with the bog. It bounced and steadied under a streaky dark sky. A full wind drove the rain horizontal. It was piercing and freezing. Prentice had used his chance to grab his bicycle and move to the far side of the truck. A door of the upturned car burst open and he saw the pink Stetson and then another tiny version of the same hat come out in a torrent. The truck engine had stopped and the only sound was the wind, the rain and through it all O'Malley singing a twisted version of a new song. 'Oh daddies, don't let your babbies grow up with bad cowgirls...' Then it was all carried away in a massive bluster of air. As Prentice made away in the storm, he noticed the passenger door of the silver truck was gouged with red.

A coal-black ceiling pressed down and the wind and rain whipped away in a ferment. He barely managed to draw a breath as he cycled up the valley. It was a demented ride. He thought of devils flying, the end of time. The whistling of the grasses and the wire gave over to the shrieking of the truck that was coming up somewhere behind him. He tried to shout out but it was snatched away in the tumult. He threw himself into the ditch and turned to see the road glimmering as the headlights flashed closer. Then there was something standing on the road. A shape. A horse. It was still and waiting between Prentice and the swelling light. Just as the truck came up, the animal turned and reared-up, a proud thing. Its coat blazed orange in the wash of the rain and the lights and he thought he saw its eyes in some triumph before it twisted away towards the truck. There was a terrible screeching and a mass of black. Everything was extinguished. Only the wind mourned on. Irish John Prentice managed at last to lift his head and make his own sound. He wondered would it wake him and take him from this land of pirates and cowboys. These badlands.

And he promised, in the streaming ditch, as he gulped for a steadying thought, to go back to his steel strings and live only in the music that he knew might turn the tables. Forget all about O'Malleys and mothers and false light. Back in the City of Blades.

COMING HOME

The traffic crawled out of Dublin, winter rain pounding the windscreen of Lizzie Kelliher's ancient red Saab. The evening was just turning to pitch and the lightscape of lamps and beams intensified from a gentle glow to a piercing glare. As soon as she had cleared the traffic lights at Newlands Cross, she checked in the mirror, spotted a gap, and moved into the fast lane. She was on the road home to Cork. The day had been lousy in every way. Her head ached. She turned the radio on to get the six o'clock news. Syria dominated. Worse for them she figured, and switched the dial to Lyric FM for some music. It was a slow, sparse jazz piece. Soon her twitchy feelings were drawn into the desultory rhythms of the music. It was a nervous harmony. She let it play.

*

The economic crash had been hard but she was slowly building again, specialising in bankruptcy. Some of her work as a forensic accountant was with the Criminal Assets Bureau, identifying and recovering the proceeds of crime. There was misery and danger, threats. That's how she'd spent the day.

She had tentatively texted home, as she drove out of the city.

Hiya. Hitting the road home now.
Earlier than expected. Hope all ok

Hello? Come in Cork.

Home life had wilted in the shade of her working life. Keeping bread on the table. Flor, her husband, was a dreamer. He told stories, jokes, morning, noon and night: a one-man variety show, and a steady job was not part of his repertoire. Him and his baldy head and his goatee—the Guns and Roses inked on his back. Spent his days up at the leisure centre displaying his tattoo, blathering with off-duty Eastern European security men and retired policemen. Lizzie had gotten tired of it all.

*

Flor was a full-time dad, but that didn't include a whole lot of work around the house. The boys, Rory and Jimmy, were both still in their teens and like their father they were rockers, leather-clad muso-heads.

The previous evening Flor had announced that he'd be off fishing in the morning.

'Bat from the Leisure has us booked for the day in Ballycotton. Boatman Bat we call him. He's —'

'In this weather? At this time of year? Jeez. You do know I'm in Dublin all day, for a case?' As usual, Lizzie had to force the odds.

'Sure hon. I'm sorry, I forgot like. Look it's not a problem. I'll take the lads for a pizza later. Might go to a film. This thing *Cloud Atlas* that's on in the Savoy. Weren't the CGIs in *Source Code* amazing?'

'Yes Flor, I get it. Just make sure they do eat. And while you're at it, the bomb-site?'

The smoke from an earlier eruption still hung in the air. 'Food' money had been used to get Jimmy a new iPhone and she'd found unopened post in a bin.

'Aw fuck it, Flor. There are bills there. How do you think this works? By CG fucking I?'

'I'm sorry, babe. I know you like it all neat around like. I should have spotted the post stuff.'

'Stuff? And neat is paying the bills!'

Rows flared often — literally, when DVDs got thrown in the fire.

*

Before Flor, Lizzie had never known a whole pile about men, useless or otherwise. She'd seen life up in a small village: herself and her mother. The family nun sorted out her education. One night in Sir Henry's brought Flor to her. Here was this funny man who could spin her some happiness while she got herself qualified. There'd been the years of festivals, fields and tents all over the country. It all fused into marriage and a slow descent into a bleak Cork suburb. The crash did for the laughter. She didn't want any more jokes. It was a dangerous time.

'Aw babe. Go easy, right? You're wired, like... out there, sorting out the underworld, or whatever. But we're here, like. All us boys we love you. Peace and love, like.'

Peace and love. Boys. Sure like. Flor managed to twist everything into some blather.

*

By Naas the jazz had given way to the soothing strings of a symphony and the road spun out, emptier. The rain too had lightened and her head had begun to clear.

She ran some more thoughts of home. Truth be told, she hated the way Flor and the boys seemed to manage so well without her now, the way they were a unit. They always seemed to be laughing at something, keeping her at bay. Making her hold back too. They left notes for her or sent her texts. A birthday reminder, exams, a gig. She sent them texts. Arrangements about coming and going, promises. Drifting, and she didn't know how to stop it.

The boys had turned on her again that morning.

'No Ma, you don't get it do you? Why do you hate Da so much? You're the disaster, like.'

She had left with those words ringing in her ears. She switched the radio off.

*

The assets-of-crime world had begun to make her jumpy. The case earlier had been typically ugly. It had involved a real lowlife, and he had been very unhappy with the way things went. Her evidence was going to make that clown very broke. The rule was to try and avoid all contact, but he had managed to eyeball her. Cold laughter in the eyes. It had frightened her. He was a stubby little white-haired specimen, out after a long sentence for drug dealing. He had managed his empire from his cell and she had just helped snatch his 'retirement' fund. Lizzie shivered away the sight of him.

She struggled with the AC system to see if she could expel the mugginess in the car. She was dressed for court today, her black suit, good blouse and heavy woollen tights, but she had to keep the heat on 'high' to clear the fog from the inside of the windscreen. There was some malfunction in the auto controls, so she fought with the dials. It never worked. Perspiration was becoming a problem. To add to all that, it had darkened considerably, away from the city, and she had been coming against traffic driving in on full beam. Her head ached again. She needed to stop.

There was a place she remembered, just off the motor-way. A rest, something to eat, wouldn't take long. So she pulled off near Portlaoise, and tried another text to Flor from the car park of the Heath Hotel.

*Weather crap. Shattered. Stopping
at heath. Rest and bite. Be late.*

The Heath was a typical new-build sort of place— went up in the boom days when every crossroads in the country got a new hotel. She had been there once be-fore, about ten years previously, at the height of all the building madness. They had stopped, the four of them, giddy, on a summer Sunday after a trip to Dublin. The place was new then and a buzz for the boys, who ordered chicken goujons and chunky chips. They had laughed at the 'posh' menu. Flor told yarns.

Now the muzziness of the lobby and the dulcet strains of piped music gave the place an air of transience. Like a very large waiting room. She slid into a banquette seat in the empty dining area. There were no other cus-tomers. The lighting was concealed and diffuse. There was a low lamp with a dark red shade on the table. She held the shiny purple cardboard affair that was a cocktail menu under the light and squinted to read it. A pinky neon glow defined the bar area over at a far wall. It was empty. A long mirror with shelves ran behind a brushed steel counter. The shelves held a sparkling array of blue, green and clear glass. A silent television flashed from a high corner. Headlines from Syria scrolled across the bottom of the screen. A young waiter in a white shirt

and black tie headed her way in an awkward hurry. He
handed her a menu.

'Evening madam. We have a special deal on a meal and
a drink. Would madam like to order a cocktail?'

She found the tone funny. Like Flor taking the piss.
She was reminded of exotic places like Copacabana,
Casablanca. Flor talk. Exotic for her was just somewhere on her own, a space to herself. She knew it was
ridiculous, and this place just a little more than a kip,
but hell, a little cocktail? Why not? One would be okay.
She would eat something. She ordered a Manhattan and
a toasted cheese sandwich. Posh.

A couple of men in suits had come in and were in
conversation over at the bar. The waiter headed off
behind the counter, and a few words were exchanged
with the men as he passed. After a moment or so, they
turned to look over in her direction. She pretended not
to notice, and didn't feel the need to put on any face.
They were a good thirty feet of dull space away.

She took her time with the sandwich and the drink
and began to chill a little. The two men were talking,
laughing and casting the odd glance her way. After a
while, she got the feeling that the looks in her direction
were becoming more meaningful, had more intent. It
made her self-conscious. And alert. She texted the boys.

Recording breaking bad? x

No responses to her texts home. That wasn't unusual,
but it still hurt. She had to make the hurt stop. Was it
worth another try? She had nearly blown it for good,

once. What was it two, three years ago now? The lads were well into secondary. Quite a wobble, her near affair. Is that what it would have been? A near miss — yes, in blind and out fast. Nothing much had happened but she had felt terrible, guilty even. The ball in her court now. Go one way or the other. Start again. In this kip? Why not?

'I'd like another one of those please.'

She placed the empty glass on the counter and turned toward the bathrooms. The tall younger man in the smart suit looked directly into her eyes as she passed, behind him the other one buried his face. The man, whose gaze now chased her, looked good in the flashy light of the bar. His eyes reflected bottle-green in a tanned face. He lounged, lithe and muscular, his white shirt open at a taut neck. Long tapering fingers held a narrow glass, like a pencil. Both men were chuckling now. Their amusement followed her to the bathroom. The mirror lights in the little room were soft, and she was surprised at the woman that looked back at her. A tired-looking woman with a lot of a life before her. If she could get it together. Maybe she could. Maybe. Those thoughts echoed. She used the door to the reception and asked about a room. There would be no problem. She sent a text.

> *Wrecked. Thinking of staying here.*
> *Thinking. C u tomorrow*

She returned by the bar, keeping her eyes to herself. The murmur from the two men rose again to a spiky snigger as she passed.

'The gentlemen say it's on them.' The waiter had his

hands flat on the bar.

'Actually, I would prefer to pay for it myself.' She kept her eyes on the waiter.

His hands stayed put.

'Put it on my bill, please.' She took the drink back to her table.

She looked up to see that the good-looking one had moved halfway across to where she sat. He stared coldly at her from a dim spot and she knew that he wasn't smiling.

'You won't take a drink from us?' He spoke quietly, matter of fact.

She didn't respond.

The older man was coming out of the shadow behind him. He reached up and, as he came by, brushed his hand on the shoulder of the other man. The lights from the bar behind created a penumbra effect around this advancing figure, and she could not see his face until he came into the lamplight near her table. He stopped beyond arms-reach. She thought she recognised something in the uplit, leery features, the pale eyes, the white floppy fringe high up on the brow. The perspiration. The wide chalky pinstripe of the suit. It was not someone she knew... although... She shivered.

*

The rain had stopped. A spare, sulphurous light fell from a high lamp standard on the vast sodden tarmac outside. There were only two cars: her old red thing and beside it a big black Mercedes. She hurried across the splashy surface and secured the locks as soon as she sat in. She had heard no sound behind her. Two shadowy figures stood staring out from the lounge window. The waiter was standing in the brightness of the hotel porch, his arms half-raised in a question. She looked towards the car park exit. The sky was now a blaze of stars and all earthly things were in sharp outline. Nothing had its really bad face on.

She texted Flor.

Changed mind. On the road home
again. Any stories hey? xx

DRESSED FOR THE KILL

The night we said our real good-byes (after I'd pulled your sodden, lifeless bodies from the river), I kissed your stony brows and then I clasped the hands of our neighbours. The women, in shock, pressing with their fingers and stroking. The knotty hands of men who had laboured their drawn-out days in workshops and fields. Hands that had dragged the river. For these are our people. The men came that night in crisp, clean clothes — clothes that men of no other station could ever wear so beautifully. Whitest of collars on weather-beaten necks and on their faces the marks of the tears that no one could shed again, for there was no longer the fight in them, or the energy. A night when every man and woman lost.

I set three iron crosses on your dry-land graves. Forms I'd forged from the remnants of a gate. One cross I decorated with a blue glaze, for you, my wife; the others I could only decorate with grief, for our daughters— too young to have understood their mother's action. I recalled the last words I'd spoken as you'd prepared to take them to the river to end your helplessness and take away their hopeless futures.

'Put on that blue dress. It suits you. Girls, it might rain. Coats. Be careful near the river. When will you be back?'

You didn't answer. You couldn't. The girls saw no need. Each word of mine must have been a dart in your exhausted head. But there was nothing: nothing left, so you put on your nice clothes. You did that so carefully, knowing that no matter how much it meant to me, you would never do it again. And then you picked up the weighted bags and left.

*

Can you hear me now? I dream. For that is what you are: a dream — my dream. My flooding memory. I'm beyond knowing what voice you hear, but I hope it's mine that you can conjure up.

*

The autumn light fades on the slip to the river. I can imagine you would say, 'Dan, you look beautifully awkward in that navy suit.' The suit I bought in Wall's Menswear for Bridgie's wedding (I didn't go — couldn't without you). The suit swims on my tightened frame — there's hardly a pick on my bones now — but my polished black shoes, ironed white shirt and scarlet tie have me turned out well. My jet hair is combed 'stunning smart', as you might say, and pulls taut off my temples. I heave and wrangle the clumsy yoke of a boat, expertly, with my calloused craftsman's hands 'til it tips the water and buoys up sulkily. I slide in that sleek gun. Long-barrelled. For ducks? I wonder. Then I step over from the sour vetches and tangles of cow parsley, and edge in. (I hope you dream now of Mary's Gold and Lady's Smock from your last Maytime). Then quickly countering the momentary bucking, I'm off in a smooth thrust into the black flow.

I float, under stars I can barely see, into a low fog settled like brushed grey wool between the banks. There are a few lights from the town winking through, but they soon disappear as I nip astride the slow midstream and drift away on it. Paddling for the old mill pond, my thoughts tick fateful and numb. All that was left has been taken away. I'd thought those days were gone, yet once again the darkness pooled inside you. An infinite black spring. It took you and our girls to the river — like cyanide.

There's some weak light on the big bend, below the cow pastures, where the current begins to charge on the short bank. The dilapidation of the old mill looms, massive and abandoned, bats darting from its gloomy eyes. A tangle of willow and ash pours out from the bank, the leaves reflecting a filtered moon. Shrubby trees grow taller on the shore and the heavier branches bend to touch the water further out, forming a hidden bower. I know these passages and tip the paddle, steering in.

There, leaning into a mossy wall of stone, out of the nervy current, I come to rest. I could be a ghillie from a nineteenth-century melodrama come to bring some other sad life to its doom, but there is only my own life to ferry now. In this forlorn place, form and shape only blink in the murk, but I manage to slip into tune with an ancient solitude. Steady once again, with a hand on the cool wall, I struggle to form a thought.

Threading fingers in the inky water I try to picture you. The day we brought our eldest, Lucy, home. That bright Spring day you wore the pale-green cotton, printed with tiny daisies. Your hair bounced — 'like a field of ripe corn' I'd said. I feel something soft — a fern frond, from its shape. I break it and bring it up to cool my lips and eyes. Outside the currents push on. Images of that last day form: what you'd worn; what they'd worn; the look in all your eyes. You went down in the Barrow water and your bodies were just breaths, cold lozenges. And your hair a freezing wind. And with you went the clock.

In this cavern of dripping stone and withering leaves, there is a sudden unease. The river rips impatiently at the roots in the bank. The branches shiver in an unsteady rhythm. Something live rustles in the undergrowth above my head. My imagination soughs. Eddies snap around some submerged affair, a paddle-reach out. A fallen trunk? Maybe I could anchor on it? A drowned pipe gives no sway when I pull hard to it. Tying up at the bow, the stern pulls slowly about and I am brushed through the branches that conceal me from the big flow outside. The cot settles in the camouflage, the air quietens and I lie flat on the hard boards, nerves calmed. It is then I hear the song.

Faint at first, I hear the broken notes (of love or agony I wonder) rise and fall on some uneven path on the other side. For a moment the breeze has thinned the fog, and through the leaves I can see a figure hobble into view as it courses the far bank. The shape in the gloaming is a short gimping entity; a soul in private abandon singing to the skies. There is a song buried deep within me too. It is in that lightless place where my soul still floats, unreachable. The fog closes in again.

There's something else coming now, on the water. It can only be imagined, for as yet there is no shape or sound. I sense it though, and invent the phantom and the noise. The fog begins to swirl, making its own matter and music. I can feel it — whatever it is that is approaching — looming large and promising.

I reach to the floor of the boat to feel for that oily barrel. Caress the walnut stock. What I do know is that I'm not afraid, not anymore. I'm prepared for whatever might be coming, nothing can be feared. First a prayer? — but I have forgotten that. Through the fog upstream, the steeple reaches aimlessly to the sky.

There's a call from a river bird and what sounds like

the movement of wings. The darkness lightens — *this time it is artificial. The flapping is louder and persistent; the sound of an engine. A throbbing areola takes shape in the gloom. The spectre has come real. (Had I truly expected this? Or was I surprised? Even now I wonder, in my own drowned realm). Deck lights suspended from poles illuminate the river cruiser. This pleasure-boat noses towards me, seeking out the pool at the river bend. It is a big affair, out of the port of Ross, and has come up the river to the tidal reach, just here. The engine is cut and its echo fades. The big boat has come about slowly and is settling side-on to my hide. Voices can be heard, and a splash as an anchor is dropped. There's an awning stretched over the deck and I can see the outlines of revellers and hear their laughter. As the cruiser drifts to a halt, ever closer, I begin to make out the human forms. Faces flicker in the bulb light sifted through the laden air. Close enough for me to make out the gaudiness of their owners. They are partying.*

Something of my old capacity has now come back as I stare out unseen from my leafy battlement. And my anger hums. But never has my mind felt steadier, more anchored. *The couple of dozen faces I find are familiar. Pale, fleshy. A liverish wash over the whole chattering fuss. The lemon women with their beady looks and jolly dresses. The louche men that like to think they run the show. That fat little man, all jowl and pinstripe, is bellowing out — laughing no doubt at his own joke — and the sound is carried to the fields beyond. I wonder about the hurt ears of cattle. These people are sure-footed and the river has become a tetchy listener, giving float to their bob and babble.*

As a child I marvelled at the skills in men's hands.

The deft flicking of the trowel, the steady touch of fingers centering a shaft, the wristy power on hay-fork, spade or hurl. A safe perch too for feather and tiny bone, or a pumice to the scratching lips of soft young life. There was a line I saw from fingertip to brain. I took this as my guide and went that way, working and shaping metal as my gift and my honest means. A means so hideously betrayed. My touch redundant. Yes, and you, in your darkness, clutched that iron last and weighted the girls, wishing they could have been spared. But not here. Not for this. And I had to let you go. Now I am free to go too.

I quietly reach down for the long gun; my feather-light breath condenses on the cold barrel as I set it onto the bow rest I'd forged myself. I slip the mooring and push out, lying on the damp floor squinting down a sight-line. My mind takes a deadly twist and my finger makes a soft move; rests easy on the eager curve of the trigger. In faded light an aim is often best. There is less glare and distraction; fewer competing nodes of brightness. *The shapes on the stilled deck cast shadows, one on the other, as they move around. Facial features oscillate. I can pick out the whole assembly against the surrounding grey.* My gimlet eye. And my dream of our eternity begins.

The crack and the visual splatter are a shocking density. Each tiny shot carries on to a place of destruction. Vermillion dots appear on the light bulbs. A haze of ripped flesh, hair and fabric swell and float. A bloody evening dust. All is shrill and then slowly there is silence as I slip out into the eternal rushing water, flies to catch.

*

If we have any memory still, is it of our girls' soft hands
nervously clutching their iron weights, our grief reflected
in their frightened eyes? Is it of the emptiness of wet tiles
in the hall? Is it of the adamant songs of better days,
when to work was to live and living was for the joy of it?
Of a time when all did not seem a confused middle, blind
to dirty advantage. Or is it of our girls' drenched corpses
dragged from Miss Barrow's watery chambers? Their
terror over for good. Maybe I can recall the impulse that
pressed that trigger? Black. And then the red splatter —
on the dangling bulbs? That dream. Poppies, sleep, for us
all.

GUACAMOLE

It all came to a head a few years back, the day Cosima died. Tiernan Robinson had his head in a book, as he ate and spoke to his wife.

'This walnut salad is delicious with the guacamole. And the vinaigrette is spot on. Where'd you learn that?'

Sally Robinson's mind was elsewhere, wondering about something else entirely.

'I couldn't find the strychnine. It's not in the usual place. There's rats in the shed.'

'Amoral creatures must know their place in the world. It's on the top shelf. Out of harm's way.' He went on with his reading. 'This Death Doula stuff is really interesting. It's quite philosophical.'

Sally didn't hear the last bit. She was thinking only of her cat, Cosima.

Sally and Tiernan Robinson had been on different pages for virtually all the sixty years of their married life. To be accurate, they were actually *on* the same page as regards one thing: they'd agreed long since that it would be a good thing if they could die together while attending a classical music performance.

'So if we could arrange to pop off together at a concert, neither of us would be left to have to tell any lies about the other.' Sally had been reading an obituary Tiernan had written for an academic colleague.

'Rightio. Agreed. And that will prove how considerate and egalitarian I am. Making sure we are both in a happy frame of mind. Listening to live music.'

Although this pact had no definite means or time frame, it was accepted that only in such a circumstance might they, with some satisfaction, bid adieu to each other and the world.

*

They'd first met when he was a young lecturer and she was a college secretary who'd typed the manuscript for his first book *Language and the Abyss*. She'd told him she followed his argument but wondered was it possible to deduce a more promising future? He'd looked patronisingly over his glasses and engaged her with a rueful reply.

'Perhaps, if you believed in those theological constructs with all their heavenly aesthetic. And *Divine Providence*. But that would need to be accompanied by prayer and that's hard on the knees.'

'Well, I'll always be praying for some sort of a heaven, where I won't need to be on my knees.' She'd laughed, as she was indeed beginning to wonder should she be giving her knees a rest. A few awkward salad teas together and she was accepting his invitation to go with him to the concerts. And she began to love the music. It allowed her to dream all those heavenly images she liked, while staying seated. He never asked her what she felt, but she thought *he* could feel something clearly. *What* he felt though, she was never sure.

One time she asked, 'What do you feel when you listen to Mendelssohn? What do you see?'

He drew a breath that seemed to take an eternity. 'I think of all the sadness in the world and try to find beauty in it.'

'And do you?'

'Do I what?'

'Find beauty?'

He turned to her and whispered, 'My struggling little Romantic.'

It gave her some comfort in the earlier years to hear such interesting and definitive views from someone whose certainties she leaned on. But what did he get from her, she wondered, besides her quiet excellence as a consoler. What matter, she tried to convince herself, sure didn't the music elevate all that was between them. She could do her own dreaming and invent new silent prayers. The more she accepted that she might never see fully into his mind, the more convinced she was that he could see right into hers. She tried not to let it disturb life unduly and hoped, and prayed that someday it would all change, be equalised. Time enough for that and it needn't have anything to do with being 'Romantic' or whatever it was that existed between them. But she knew that something needed to give. Eventually.

*

On the day after Cosima's demise, Sally resurrected the idea of the pact. Tiernan was at his desk working on a review of another book on nineteenth-century German philosophy. He raised his solemn face and said,

'Rightio. Fine. We should prepare properly so.'

Booking tickets and making speculative arrangements became a very particular preoccupation for Sally and, for many months, a routine developed and her sense of purpose grew. As did her courage. Then the pandemic came. The shut-down of all live performance brought such a frustrating commitment to survival that they'd even discussed other forms of ecstasy that might accompany their demise, but in the end nothing seemed attractive. Reading books in each other's company was satisfying but not really unifying. Listening to a recording, of say Schubert, was grand but there was no sense of the completeness you'd get with an orchestra in the Concert Hall. So when the lockdown ended and the first tickets for a live concert went on sale, Sally decided there was no way they were not going to be in that audience.

The performance was advertised as a contemporary quartet: a harpist, a cellist, a flautist and a singer who were to play in an Anglican church in the city. The programme would be some sort of fusion of the classical and the traditional. It sounded challenging and Tiernan had raised a dubious eyebrow.

'Fusion is not something I'd wish on J.S. Bach or any of his children. Certainly not from some eejit with a fiddle.'

'Oh, there's little fear of that. No fiddles. Or bodhráns. These are top classical people. And our first chance... you know... for a while.'

'Hmmh. Well okay, so long as there's no muck-savage tapping his feet, I'll give it a go. It might well be the night.'

*

Despite the moribund philosophies that dominated their home, they had always been in good health. This was in large part thanks to a dedication to a so-called Mediterranean diet and a strict avoidance of alcohol. The thinking on all this was largely — well, wholly — down to Tiernan. The single-mindedness that afflicted him never seemed to abate and Sally struggled to find echoes of her former... optimism. In essence, other than books and music, for Sally it had all descended into a terrible joy-

lessness. And the pandemic hadn't helped. She'd continued to float about him. Looked after his needs without
the need to agree or disagree. Except on the matter of
how it would all end.

*

They had gone about their preparations for the first
time in well over a year. Checking that bills had been
paid, putting out the bins, making sure the windows
were closed and all plugs were out. Sally had a few bits
of jewellery which she checked were in their usual place.
There was also an old diary with some photographs
folded in. These were items which she kept very much to
herself and was unsure what should be done with them,
after. All she could do was to leave them. So she noted
that they were safely in place in her special box. Tiernan looked over some important papers and then tidied
them and left them in a prominent place on his desk. He
straightened the family photographs that stood absolute
in their sturdy frames. His parents, the grandparents, all
well gone now, and better for it, as he'd often suggested.

As was usual she prepared his favourite snack — the
guacamole. She watched him dip the oat crackers into
the avocados she had mashed to her own recipe. It was
only when he was eating like this that she ever noticed
his elegant hands and the way they delivered the glassy
food to his lips, that were shaped into something like a
smirk after he had swallowed.

'You not eating? What do they say about how to keep a man happy? Well, I'm a happy man.'

'I had something earlier. If you've had your fill, I'll get rid of the rest. Don't want to be leaving a mess.'

'Rightio. Good. I hope the music lives up to it. But I'm not convinced about the chances of our imminent mutual demise. Too much hope around.'

'It will be cold in the church. Better wear a coat.' Sally, as always, spoke with a quiet resignation as if for the two of them. Tiernan, who never gave the impression he was listening, made a barely audible comment. 'Damn shoe polish where the hell...' and then, as was his wont, went on to loudly make his own proposition. 'I think we should wear coats. It might be over the top for July but it would be a smart move. Yes. And I think you should wear woolly socks. You can't rely on the Prods.'

'What do you mean ?'

'Too mean. To turn on the heat. Or too broke. Should say "Expect Draughts" on the tickets.'

'Aren't Catholic churches just the same?'

'Wouldn't know. They don't have concerts. Too well-off.'

'Whatever it is, I don't want it to be from the cold. That would be an uncomfortable way to go out.'

'Well your feet will be warm.'

'Isn't that what they say about Hell?'

'Wouldn't know. Haven't quite got a handle on that place yet.' He let out a baleful snigger, as much as his manner and frailty allowed.

They debated the chances of their catching a chill and agreed that would not be in keeping with the idea of a comfortable doze-off into eternity. So it was decided that they would wear coats. And wear wool socks, bring hats, gloves and scarves — just in case. And Sally added her final remark on the matter.

'An umbrella too. Whatever about the cold, I'm not going to die wet.'

Before they headed out, she filled a saucer of milk and left the carton back in the empty fridge, a drop for a cup of tea. Tiernan pulled the hall door closed behind them and immediately opened it again. He went back into the hall and straightened the picture of the Hero S. He stood back, seemed satisfied and came out again. This Hero's name had not been mentioned in years, as Sally didn't approve of any of his heroes, but Tiernan was allowed to be steadfast and, although secretly he had lost a little faith in S, he wanted it there as some sort of a spur. A signal maybe. Only he knew of things that he was uncertain about.

As usual they walked to the tram stop and nodded slightly in the direction of anyone they passed that deserved recognition. Thanks to the politeness of some students, they sat on opposite seats but the proximity of standing passengers and the masks were enough, if needed, to dampen any conversation. Tiernan closed his eyes while Sally absorbed the city landscapes as they glided by.

They walked from the tram to the church through warm streets that were crowded with young people drinking, and Sally watched the sun perform a last tease of the day. She spotted a bin and some young women stood aside to allow her dump the umbrella. The women quietened and looked slightly confused as the old pair in their winter coats shuffled off again. Sally and Tiernan communicated in the din by gestures but they knew where they were going. She carried on slowly with her thoughts, privately honed again in anticipation of what they were about.

Outside, as they approached the steps of the church, Sally was surprised by the numbers gathered. Inside, they were shown to a wooden pew a couple of rows from the front. The hard upright backs caused them to bend forward, their bodies unable to fit the form of these benches. An attentive young man came with some cushions. Tiernan fixed him with a patronising stare and then spoke in a weak voice that came across as ironic.

'Well, I hope the music doesn't undo the comfort of this cushion.'

The young man gave him a smile, then signalled that he should adjust his mask and, glancing quizzically at Sally, went away to continue his duties. The atmosphere was warm enough so Sally helped him off with his coat and settled him. She then removed her own coat, studied the programme and chided him.

'They are all very good players. Try and not let the form bother you and you never know.'

'There isn't a single thing here I recognise. What am I supposed to make of a title like *Cuachán*? How do you even pronounce it?'

'Sssshh.' Sally leaned over as just then the performers came out to relieve the pent-up expectation of the packed church.

The quartet quickly quietened the applause as they settled with their instruments. The singer, a slight man with a closely shaven head, seemed to recognise Sally as he settled behind a small desk with a computer. It made her feel self-conscious. The man began an introduction in a low-toned chatty voice. There was occasional laughter from the audience as he spoke. Tiernan spoke out in a loud voice.

'I can't hear you.'

Sally reached over to press his hand and raised her finger to her lips. That didn't stop Tiernan but he lowered it to a whisper.

'What's he going to do with that computer yoke? I hope this isn't some electronic thing.'

He leaned forward to hear better and it caused his frame to sink further in the pew. Sally leaned with him and they perched like two old birds: one in a pale blue cardigan, one in a faded linen jacket—both garments stretched taut over old bones.

The singer started up with an old Irish air and the instruments sparingly suggested the melody. The sound was restrained and gentle, the harpist finding strong single notes as punctuation. Tiernan's instinct was to straighten up and regain his pose but he couldn't seem to manage that against the strain of his position and Sally, conscious of his struggle, stayed with him. As the song came to an end, the players moved without interruption and developed the air into an increasingly jaunty tune, the women leading on harp and flute and the cellist finding his space with some classically formed contrapuntal passages. Gradually and imperceptibly, the Robinsons leaned further forward so that from behind, Sally thought, they might appear to be shrinking in their pew.

A couple of more pieces followed, slower and very much bigger, as each instrument stated its own authority with confidence. Sally was gradually transported and, along with the old stone and stained glass, wrapped in to a musical space that seemed to reach out for her spirit. All the while she and Tiernan sank deeper in their places. Suddenly, the music stopped and, after a pause, something vastly different could be heard. It was quite faint at first but there was clearly a drone of single notes swelling. The players had rested so it wasn't from the instruments that this sound came, but the singer was coolly operating some buttons on his laptop. There were faint ethereal sounds, the scratchy bare sound of a fiddle rising, falling, starting, stopping and then some voices — ghostly it seemed. Chatterings from times gone. The singer added his own enigmatic tones. The language was ancient but was newly refreshing on a melody; the words were strange and unintelligible but evocative; the notes were from another world. The whole of it somehow took shape and opened for Sally as a capsule from the past. A mesmerising sound dream.

She didn't want it to end. From the corner of her eye, she saw that Tiernan had let his body drop forward just about as far as it could go. His mask had slipped and there was an ironic smile sealed on his lips. She knew this should have shocked her, but no, she continued in the reverie. As the piece played on, she reached over and let her hand rest on Tiernan's back. There was no movement but she was happy he was in a good balance. She allowed her thoughts travel back with the music into the vaults. There was something there for her and she knew the music would never stop now. She reached over again with her handkerchief and wiped a fleck of dried guacamole from the corner of his mouth, shaking out the cloth with a sudden vigour. Then she rested her fingers gently on his lips. She sensed that his blood may not be flowing anymore. His eyes finished the story for her. She hoped he'd found the stillness of the far shore. She'd be happy for him there. Something new for him. A place where only phantom tempers exist and the eternal echoes of any concerto can be accommodated to the harshest of spirits.

Sally tried to remember where she had left her umbrella, whether there was milk for tea. Had she disposed of the rest of the guacamole safely, she wondered. She tried to run her mind over a myriad of things that would be left to do. But gradually the murmuring ended and there was only the droning note. She looked up at some numbers in frames. Psalms, or was it hymns? She thought that they were displayed with a palpable certainty. This awareness gave her a frightening comfort.

She looked forward to a glass of wine. And feeding the new cat that she'd soon have. There was nothing much else to think about. For the moment.

THE WOMAN ON THE BUS

Galway Bay radio is always there in the background when I'm in the house. I rang in once but hung up before they answered. It was a thing that I was going to say about what started on the bus. But on second thoughts, no. Sure, if there was someone listening...

*

My husband died before the conservatory was finished. Now it's just bare blocks, gravel floor, no roof and no glass. Men are odd. They're mostly likeable but you can't let them get too close: then they mightn't be who you thought they were. Oh, there are plenty of them around but I don't let them in. Well not after... not since. I'd always be happy with a how're-you-doing from Matt, the postman—he always reminds me of the thin fella with the glasses in *Circle of Friends*—or a wave from some old guy passing on his bike. A lot of Galwaymen look like Robert De Niro. All the men I see remind me of someone who was in something or other. The lad that drives the bus looks like Barry Fitzgerald. Jimmy Burke up on his tractor could be Robert Mitchum. There's no end of resemblances. And they aren't all old Hollywood men either. Sure amn't I fully up to date with the younger ones. TV. *Poldark*. And around Galway. Don't I go all the time to see the Druid. I spend my life watching men. Actors. I wonder sometimes am I living in the real world at all.

*

I used to be the woman on the bus. Mondays: 8am into Galway for the shopping and then back again by lunchtime. See the tourists swarming around Joyce's in Moycullen, looking for the green marble. Steal a glance over the wall at Glenlo Abbey. Its Pullman restaurant and all. Now, there'd be a place for the Hollywood lads.

It'd be dark waiting on winter mornings but in spring there might be a flash of a thrush on the ditch. That hedge runs all the way to the lane for Burke's farm. Malachy Molloy across never lifts a blind until I'm well gone, and the cast from his yard light doesn't even reach the road at the blackest hour. Malachy lives above his lounge bar directly over from me, and it's the only other building on this stretch. I've never set foot in Molloy's. I see all the stars coming and going though.

*

It was a Monday, one of those blank November days. You'd hear the shotguns go off in the woods up behind. I'd been on the early bus as usual and was back home and in the kitchen. There was a song about teenage love playing on the radio. I was slicing carrots for soup and thinking of teenagers and how very different they seem now to the ones I used to teach. There is something very impressive about the way the flesh of a carrot resists before it gives in. Mind you, I have the sharpest of blades. My Sabatier steel never loses its edge. The kitchen looks out through a glass sliding door at the back of the house. That door was put there to get more light from the new conservatory, but with the way it's ended up there's more of a gloom coming in. There's a garden beyond that can be lonely, and sure I'd let it grow over a good bit. Anyway, there I was lopping away, thinking of young life, and I looked up and there he was at the glass. A man I'd never seen before, not looking in at me but not quite looking away either. I froze on the spot, holding the butt of a carrot in one hand and the knife-edge to the chopping board in the other, my elbow raised. I was so shocked that I forgot how to open my mouth and so whatever I was feeling, the fright, the thrill, just tremored down through me. When I finally found my voice again, my legs had gone so weak that all I could think about was collapsing, so I let out a sound like a long *oh*. A woman in her eighties with my slight frame might never rise again I thought. But I didn't fall and by the time I'd caught my breath back, I saw that this man had pressed in to face me full-on and seemed to be saying something. My hearing was gone with the shock, like a bomb had gone off, and the idea of the next explosion — my hearing returning in a rush of sound, like I'd seen in the films — had me all scrunched up. I tapped the knife on the chopping board and I heard that clearly, so of course I knew then that I just couldn't hear him through the glass — the double glazing. That relaxed me a bit and gave me some go-on, despite the terrifying sight of a man with a torn face mouthing something, perhaps shouting, in at me at the back of my own house and no one to protect me. My first collected thought of course was to run out of there, my own kitchen. But where to? And, for a reason I couldn't remember, I was wearing my brown town hat and my short Wellingtons. Good that my teeth were in though. The next thing that came into my head was to get the front door properly locked. I knew the back was locked because I'd done it earlier, before I went out to the bus. There was a very good locking system on that one. I wasn't feeling so sure about the front though. Funny the things that go through your head. I started to wonder if I'd fed the cats! Did I expect help from a bunch of hungry cats? Then I saw that he was holding up something, a book, and pointing at it. He seemed desperate that I pay attention. Somehow the sight of the book blew off some of the fear — I figured he wasn't about to break in and slaughter me with a book. Careful now, I reminded myself. So, never taking my eyes off him, I stepped back and fumbled on the kitchen counter trying to find my panic button. It was supposed to be around my neck but it never was. My hand rested on my watch, which I'd taken off earlier when I was washing the carrots.

I held it up, concealed in my hand, and pointed at it as if I was going to press it. He shrugged and raised his hands as if to say alright you win and I'll be off. There was something vulnerable in his expression and gestures. Not evil. More sad. Childlike even. He reminded me of someone... He held the book up again slowly, and appealed to me, with his blob-by-looking eyes, to look at it. I moved my finger back from the hidden watch, jabbed towards it again to remind him, grabbed hold of the sweeping brush, and then took the first couple of steps so's I could see better. He seemed to smile and gave a little thumbs-up sign. I had to lean forward to make out the title of the book. *Crime and Punishment.* Jesus. I half stumbled backwards again and my hand went up to my mouth. He was vigorously shaking his head. I was back in even more shock now. That was the book I was reading.

He put the book away in a pocket and stepped back a little, his hands doing the calm-down thing. I needed to hear something so I reached up with the brush and opened a small window over the sink. A silence came rushing in with the scent of rotting leaves and then a soft, rich kind of voice.

'Please. Please. I don't mean you any harm.' He sounded like an actor.

'What do you want? What are you doing in my... conservatory?' I half shouted keeping my eyes on him. I saw his face was not cut but had deep lines and was weather-beaten, or was it a lack of weather, anyway it had a high colour. Who did he remind me of?

'Sorry I didn't mean to frighten you. There was no answer at the front so—'

'What do you want?'

'I saw you reading on the bus,' he tapped a pocket in

his raincoat. 'I'm reading it too. It's still a great favourite of mine.'

I hadn't noticed him on, or getting off, the bus. But I did notice now that his voice had a kind of a familiar tone to it. For some reason that eased me to a better opinion of him. I decided to keep my defences up though.

'Yes, it's a wonderful book. The moral...' I started, thinking at the same time why am I having a conversation with a man in a grubby raincoat who obviously has been watching me on the bus and has followed me into my house? Well, he had got himself as far as the conservatory. The half-conservatory. And the 'familiar' voice didn't ring that well either on second thoughts... that fella... what was his name? I really had to stop this, so I started thinking about the front door again while he went on. I hoped there might be a signal, but where was my mobile? If only I'd kept the landline in the kitchen.

'I have some business with Malachy over. When he opens. It seems he's off somewhere. So I thought I'd just pop in to you and—'

'Just pop in, is it? Well, that's nice of you but my late...' Oh, I wished I hadn't always to think of my husband as *late*. 'I'm afraid it's not very convenient just now. I—'

'Oh, I'll leave you in peace so. I just thought... oh, I don't know... I just thought, while I'm waiting, here's a chance to talk, you know, the coincidence.'

The more he spoke the more his voice got at me. Who...? Oh, get him away from here. It really bothered me that he looked so down-and-out though. I noticed his coat was waxed so I thought maybe he might be one of those old Anglo types who couldn't afford the upkeep of the estate anymore so they just descended into... shabbiness? His bedraggled appearance didn't fully hide some... quality. He had a full mouth, even a mite sensitive, and fine skin beneath the high colour. The lines were very deep, like crevices. His eyes were limpid bluey bulges and seemed honest. I made a stab at fiftyish because of the twisty grey strands in the big mop that tipped onto his craggy brow.

'You know Malachy so?' I was looking for a reference for my mister... Miley. Yes, that was it. 'You're—?'

'Oh yes. We go back. Met him when he was in Munich before he took over from his father across the way. Ran a place. You know all that. Learning the ropes. Did a few things together.'

It started to rain.

*

I made him sit at the end of the table away from the back door. His clothes were actually clean but very worn. He drank the tea and spoke politely about the convenience of the bus. It's funny the way extraordinary things can be reduced to the ordinary by conversation. (My uncle interrupted a burglar about his business in the house one night and they spent a couple of hours talking over tea about how hard it was to make a few bob). I told my man that moons ago I'd been an English teacher in the 'Jes' and tried to steer our talk back to books by saying I'd taught *Crime and Punishment* to the sixth years. He was nodding at all this, like he knew or something. It struck me as a little intimate but then with a wave of his hand he dismissed my hurried comments about women in literature and then shook his head and grimaced when I asked if he'd been reading any of the young Irish writers. Somehow, that all brought me back aways.

'Sally Rooney? Surely—' I could see the name meant nothing to him. 'But Dostoyevsky though?'

'Oh. Indeed. Himself. Yes. The very man. I suppose I'm a man for... ah sure... over the years you know... there's probably not much that hasn't already—'

'A lot yes, but the moral questions don't change, no? Great fiction chewing on philosophy. The personality of the killer? The carelessness of murder? The question of the spirit? And consequence? There's the rub. Spit it out. Kill and be damned? Or repent?' I had got all that out in a scatter but then had to halt up, considering the circumstances. He looked confused. There was definitely your man... Miley, yep, in him, but there was something else too that should have been ringing my bells a bit louder. Something familiar.

'Look you're the teacher here, I'll only embarrass myself. My schooldays weren't that great. So, what's going into the pot with the carrots?'

That reminded me and gave me the breathing space I needed. So I told him about the soup and he suggested I keep going with that and, that if I didn't mind, could he use the toilet. I told him to use the one in the hall and stood over to finish the chopping. How could all this feel so normal now, so matter-of-fact? I thought I heard the front door closing so I went to see but he was on his way back in from the hall.

'That's a lovely picture of a dog in your front room. Do you have a dog?'

I told him no, the dog was gone, but the picture was painted by a woman I'd taught who'd gone on to be a really good artist and who'd come out especially to do it a few years ago.

'Must be nice to be visited by an old pupil? A successful one?'

I was feeling quite exposed again with no husband, no dog, and no hungry cats to look out for me. I felt foolish and nervous. I put the carrots in a saucepan and the implements I'd been using in the sink before I sat opposite him again. Something had changed in him. Ever since he'd come into the house, he'd been very relaxed but now he was gathering speed. He told me his name was Mick — I nearly died on the spot — made some joke about not paying attention in class and asked me my name. He asked in a way that led me to think that this was something that might not actually interest him. He mightn't even need to hear. So I told him it was Lauren and I felt myself shiver. In fairness, I always did when I suddenly had to think of my husband, Mister Humphrey Bogart himself. His look said *oh yeah?* A look that I thought might lead to a bad turn in affairs.

'I think I heard Malachy's car. Maybe he's back.' I was glad to be able to say something fast.

'Oh good. I'll be getting on over so. Thanks so much for the tea and the catch-up. I really enjoyed it.'

He insisted on washing the teacups and then he made to leave. I showed him out the front door — he had to help with the catch, my hands were shaking so much. I saw that Malachy's door was open, so that took care of some of my wobbles. He smiled a goodbye and then strolled over and into the bar. I was left shook and racking my sorry brains. Who?

*

There was a knock on my front door at around 5 pm. It was dark.

'Who is it?'

'Malachy. Malachy Molloy.'

I recognised the voice. I switched on the porch light and opened the door very carefully. It was Malachy. He had his young Jimmy Stewart face on.

'Are you alright? These are... yours?' He seemed satisfied and reached out to hand me a book and a knife. I was stunned again. 'He said he knows you. You taught him?'

'Who...? Where...? I was looking for that knife. That's the book... I'd no idea.' Better not say, I thought.

'He had them over in the bar.'

'Who...?' I still wasn't going to say.

'Ah, he's a guy's been coming in to me. Used to be a solicitor in town. Mick something. Lonergan. Yeah. Mick Lonergan. Lost everything including... you know,' he pointed to his head. 'Had been in a couple of times before I copped it. Lot of them do, you know. Just sit there, day in, each one looking in a different direction, each one's world limited by a boundary, no-one talking. They're all barred somewhere else. It's a circuit thing. Sure, you have to have customers.'

'That sounds awful.' I was trying to imagine how

awful. Although... some of them were my actors.

'Ah, most of them are fine. In fact this guy always struck me as a really... Do you know that actor? Oh, what's his name Milo... eh no... the Druid guy... Mick... Mick Lally. Did you teach him?'

'Mick Lally? No.'

'No, I mean the chap—'

'I thought...' I caught myself on just in time. Molloy raised an eyebrow.

'You—?' he started.

'Ah nothing, I was only thinking how men... you know they, you, all look... you know... like actors. To me.' That seemed to be enough, although he did the droopy thing with his mouth again and looked curiously at me for a few moments longer than I would have liked. Then he seemed happy to go on.

'Of course. Anyway, we weren't sure what he was at with the knife. Nothing bad happened, he was waving it about. Was shouting about murder or something. "Kill and be damned." That's it. "Or repent." Yeah. Repent. That's what he said. Gave it over peaceful. Pulled the book from his pocket and waved it about too. Harmless. The fecker started to cry when he handed the book over.' Molloy paused, looked kind of pityingly at me, and then went on. 'We saw it has your, eh... Humphrey's... name on it. The Lord have mercy on him. Glad you are okay.'

I felt quite glad too.

'God I... my book. I never...' But I remembered now I'd left it on the hall table.

'Your front door was open again. When I was driving out at lunchtime. You didn't... He obviously... That's how he must've... Oh look, there's no need to worry. He's sent well on his way. Didn't want to get the Guards on him. I'll tell Fahy quietly, and he'll keep an eye. Troubles enough. He'd be back in Ballinasloe for a spell in the old days. Don't know what they do these days. I'd be happy enough he won't be back around here again anytime soon. Keep your doors locked though.'

Well I will, I thought, but then I couldn't get the word *asylum* out of my head.

'Oh god. I was feeding the cats. I must've left...'

'Mary, you've got to be more careful. 'Specially... you know... What do you say?'

*

In the end I never said. Isn't it terrible to think of how someone can slip in through a crack in your routine or imagination. Small comforts and someone sees an opportunity. And all those young men I taught. Slipping in from the past like that. How bad is that? All that stuff going on around. You'd never know who might come to your door. Strange fellows now. Like they are all... in something. Well, it's enough to make you bolt up tight. Let them all be in something. Just see them in that. And there I was about to tell the world about the day I let *him* in. Sure, who would I have said it was? I'm so glad I stopped before I made a fool of myself on the radio. Isn't it great though, the radio. Sure, how else would I have heard of The Stunning?

MISCHIEF

Oona thought the air in these hotel rooms always tasted of chemicals and this time there was a pinky-beige hue which made her think she might retch. The young man had come out of the shower with a towel around his waist and was plugging in an electric saw.

'What do you think you are doing with that thing?'

'I'm chargin' it.'

'No, I mean what's it for?'

'It's for my new act. Sawin' the Lady. In half. You know.'

'Not in here please. What if it goes off? It makes me afraid. I don't want my room filling up with body parts. That wasn't the deal. You're cleaned-up, so finish off and get the hell. I'll see you later on that street where I showed you.' Oona knew the ropes and so she knew the risks with wild young men from god-knows-where.

Everything in the room seemed to be in the usual order: tea-maker, television, ironing board and bedside lockers. She unpacked her case and filled a drawer with costumes and other paraphernalia. She placed a small box of valuables in the safe and entered her four-digit secret code: the year she claimed her grandfather had first arrived from Russia. It was also the date on the gold medal she said he had gotten from Tsar Nicholas.

She took a glass of water onto the small balcony where she could breathe a little easier and calm her nerves. The unease might have disturbed her once, but she had learned with the years to recognise and appreciate the tension that her work demanded. She needed to feel it so she could stay on it. The view out over the town of Tralee was unremarkable. Except, that is, for the Ferris wheel that stood unlit in the dull midday, at rest over the expanse of low grey buildings. Early autumn swallows skittered on telegraph wires, drumming up the energy for a seasonal departure.

*

Everyone knew Oona Sukhrova as a circus girl. She had her family story. They had been in the circuses for generations. *The Incredible Sukhrovas.* Her father and mother had died in a car crash in Donegal, one of the very first, years ago, while they were with Barrys. Like her brothers and sisters, she was looked after then by the Barrys, until she eventually went out on her own. She made a good living on the streets, at festivals and in the cities and bigger towns, building her act on her skills as a tightrope walker, juggler and fire-eater. She had worked for a while as a dancer and then as a singer in a band. All that had ended with the shooting up North. She'd been hit in the throat but survived, unlike her husband and the others. Troubled times. There was a scar now in her voice and her words sounded scolloped from exotic depths.

Tralee was to be her first appearance with this new kid, her assistant. She had hooked up with him a couple of weeks back in Thurles, where they had both tried their luck in the Square at the hurling final. His act there — *The Strongest Man in Ireland* — had been tame enough. Here was this slender, wiry kid tearing telephone books and smashing potatoes on his forehead, but there was nothing else tame about Blackbird. He got his name from her that first evening.

'You know what you are?' she had said. 'A bird. A blackbird. Do you remember that song? "Blackbird"? Learn to fly. That's what you need to do. That's who you are.'

She loved to watch him dress, sliding his tight, narrow frame into his grubby vest, greasy brown pinstripe, and ruby silk scarf. Muscular and wiry to his core, he lived on vodka, meat and raw eggs and when he gave you a look, you had to search for his dark eyes beyond the streels of black hair that hung to his shoulders. He glided on slender, tapered, bare feet and himself and Oona fell together easily. She needed a new assistant and he needed time to work up another act. Blackbird seemed wily enough for her, so they started out: she, diminutive, in her flouncy dresses and leather slippers, her green eyes and her coppery hair curled tight to her sallow scalp. Like two characters from a fairy tale.

*

In the early afternoon, Oona made her way through the teeming crowds to her performance space on Denny Street. The town was in full festival swing. Blackbird supervised the unloading of the small white van. They erected two tripods thirty feet apart and strung a wire six feet high between them. Oona came into the arena that the excited crowd had opened up for her. She was wearing a gold leotard with a matching tutu over green tights. The outfit was embedded with sparkling sequins. She stretched up a bare arm to feel the wire and then checked the stays at both ends. Blackbird worked with her in silence, attending to the necessary adjustments for anchoring and tension. He added his own bouncing authority to the proceedings. They held the audience in expectant thrall as they wound up the preparations. Oona had the last say and made the final tweaks herself. By the time she'd swung her tiny body up onto the wire, the crowd had swelled and the first outpouring of surprise and acclaim went up. She was erect on the wire now and poised. Blackbird was at his table below, ready to get her juggling clubs and fire-torches to her. A look passed between them that nobody noticed. It was that moment where they invested trust, but also revealed to each other their vulnerabilities. Her eyes focused as she settled, a series of hesitations before the natural brilliance of her action took over. His eyes were burning up like comets. In a series of lightning-fast glances, they gave courage and certainty to the precision of what was about to happen. All flaw and confusion was expressed and then eradicated in those looks, for that time anyway.

*

'So, this sawing show?'

'I'm working it up. It'll be a mighty thing.'

'Have you tried it somewhere?'

'Oh I've... well, I seen it first on the TV. It's kind of obvious. We tried it... back there... well you know. After I gave up the boxin'. After...'

'And did it work?'

'Bejaney, it was great. It'd be some show if I could really go at it. Bejaney, it would be a fine thing if I really did it.'

'You mean if you really sawed someone in half?'

'Yeah. Like one of them Roses. Cut them from the bush. And the stupid show ponies that goes with them.'

*

Blackbird took his break at a licenced premises in the far reaches of the town. He fell in with some men he'd hung out with before at various to-do's around the country. Jackmen. They were strung out the length of the small bar, mostly young, dressed in training pants and hoodie jackets. If it wasn't for the pallor and emaciation of their faces, they might have passed for a sports team of some sort. Touts. Their leader was an older, heavy-set man whose eyes were bloodshot blobs in a head crowned by a black wool hat. He sat up and gave instructions and heard reports in a language that was hard to decipher. A language of curses and twisted essentials. Between his pronouncements, he blew coins off the sodden wooden counter into an empty pint glass. Blackbird felt a coin strike the side of his own glass and then splash into the neat vodka. All around him the hum was silenced and heads turned. The faces that had been expressive and friendly now entered into an impassive ritual. The leader spoke, his tone holding out the possibility of some threat if his soft, deliberate words were to be somehow misunderstood.

'Young fella, I'm told you been up the town in right good company. Makin' a fuckin' show. Hustlin' with show folk. Huh?'

'I'm helpin' out with a...'

'Helpin' the Rushian wan. What? Helpin' yourself to what now? An' us stupid jacks all up here mindin' our own business and tryin' to mind it well.'

The man needed no effort to gather everyone in. The company had a necessary little snigger to itself. The man went on.

'How's about you started givin' a hand here? Give a bit

of your "helpin'" to your jack-mates from the Big Smoke here? That would be a better show. Huh? What are you sayin'? I'm not sure if I'm hearin' ya.'

Blackbird wasn't saying anything yet. He was looking at the copper coin sitting in the bottom of his glass, like a lozenge about to be dissolved. He spoke then in a cocky tone.

'Yeah well, I've got that Rooshian well-taped. She's carryin' a box of the most gorgeous jewels around with her. There's a gold... and who has had his eye on it this while?'

'That's an interestin' question here now. So you've to do nothin' much really. Carry on with your new show-lady is all? ' The bossman was measuring.

'Hush a bit now. That's my lot, not yours,' Blackbird blurted.

'I suppose it may be, but please tell me are you thinkin' of your brudders here too?' There was danger in the bossman's tone.

Blackbird didn't know if any of them were his brothers or his mates. But sure, they were all he had up to now. And they might be something to frighten him a bit too.

'You know men...' The bossman looked around at the others and then back at Blackbird — he looked at him in mock admiration. 'The young fella's got a thing goin' there. I'm thinkin' this here is a smart young buck. What about it, men?'

There was a rumble of good-natured approval until a growl came up from the leader as he leaned in towards Blackbird, fixing him with a most terrible stare.

'Of course, don't fuckin' forget our share. And what you were bred for. You pup. Later, when they are all above

in that Dome, them Roses and the lads that do be mindin' them, and everyone watchin' 'em — that's when we'll
be out to play. We'll expect you on the pitch and in the
game so?'

Blackbird felt a numbness creeping from his toes and
up to his knees: a familiar weakness when he was unsure
of his ground. He wondered what ground he needed to
stand on to keep things right for himself.

*

'Nowhere that I can remember.' Oona was telling Blackbird where she came from. 'Might be nowhere at all. Sure,
where do any of us come out of? It's probably right that
we are left down somewhere, might as well be, by some
great bird. Who's going to mind our eyes when the time
comes is a better question.' Oona saw that Blackbird had
rolled his own eyes as she posed all that. Was he trying to
imagine blinding or plucking she wondered. He answered,
'They used leave coins on the eyes. Was that to protect
them?'

'Money for the Ferryman.'

'Don't think the ferryman above in Tarbert got paid
that time...'

'What time?'

'Ah, I think I'd a family that travelled a bit. Never
mind. Seagulls pluck anythin' loose from that ferry. Anyway, I'm a sort of nowhere-man too. Though they say I was
maybe born in Limerick some-kinda-wheres. I like it that

I don't have a place to come from. Like you. We can do better shows. Not carin' like.'

'I wouldn't go around "not carin" too much,' she said, 'but maybe you've got something there. Maybe it's not being all that bothered. In my life I've never been much bothered about, say, what might be happening to other people. Live and let live — good and evil — so long as nobody's getting murdered. Not too many give a fuck, but I won't ever forgive murdering. Other mischief yeah, but not murdering.' She took a few moments to compose. 'May those murdering fuckers burn.'

Blackbird had come back to the room to pick up his saw. He was sitting at the end of the bed, watching her undo herself after the day. She removed the sparkly grains from her face, brushed her hand across it a few times and then rubbed in a white cream for the ageing lines. He watched as she went over to the safe and took out her jewel-box. It was of hard polished wood inlaid with ivory. She took off her show earrings and put them in the small box. There were other things in there too. Valuable things. She put the box back in the safe and closed it.

'This is the only thing, other than the strength in my limbs, that I got from my folks,' she told him.

That's what had made him ask her, again, where she was from. Although he knew nothing about settlement, he thought if you had a thing like that box, you had to be from somewhere; somewhere he couldn't imagine, and maybe if you really were from somewhere, you might not care too much for bad stuff. Now he was wondering how he could keep it like that.

*

There's a moment in any show where the patter has run its course and something needs to happen. Then it's all about the burning-out of the fuse before the impossible. Impossible depends on vulnerabilities: the performer and the audience. When Houdini is handcuffed and submerged in his milk-can full of water, it's human frailty that is in play — and then, when he escapes, it is heroic, and also a kind of relief which returns everyone to a safer place, deeper within themselves.

'I need to tell you somethin'.'

Blackbird had managed to gear down his tone so Oona might listen differently. She turned from the mirror with an attention that allowed him to continue.

'You see there's these men I know and they've come down from the big city for a kinda... a kinda... makin' mischief.'

'What kind of mischief are we talking about here?' She spoke the words like she knew the measure and was trying to give it a score. 'What end of the scale? How do you know these men anyway? How does it matter to you?'

'It's robbery they're after plannin'. A pluckin' if you like. There's some of them say they're my mates. But they're right bad jacks. They want me to come in here for a start.'

'And?'

'Into the room here.'

'There's nothing here.'

'They want me to be here later. To open up when everyone's up at the Roses. They'll be lookin' for their cut. They won't trust me on me own.'

'Well, I can see what you are telling me. But what are you asking me?'

*

A time comes, once a year in that town, when a famous beauty contest is nearing its climax. The interlude before the announcement of the result is a drum-roll of minutes when the whole place holds its breath. Everything is in suspense waiting for a cue: fireworks to explode; an orchestra to play; crowds to cheer; lights to flash. Razzmatazz all set. Then the announcement. *The winner of this year's Rose of Tralee is... from Boston, Massachusetts, Mary O'Dea!* It all kicks off, the RTÉ orchestra plays to a chorus of thousands singing the song: 'The pale moon was rising...' Fireworks blast the air into raucous colour.

At that very moment, the door to the hotel room is quietly opened and a man steps into the gloom — the night outside crackling. A figure is sitting on the bed, in shadow so only the reflections of the green and gold explosions outside allow the intruder to be in anyway seen. The man in his beanie is shark-like. He whispers.

'Well, you did expect me now. Didn't you? Have you got it?'

The figure on the bed nods towards the safe on the

console. The safe is open. The man takes out the box, opens it and roots around until he picks something out. The broken light pattern reduces his expression to a flicker. The man now moves towards the window to get a better look at what he holds in his hand. He opens his palm towards the light-bursts outside, and sees the gold medal, nestled like his fortune. The racket is too loud, and he's too excited to hear the revs of the saw as it travels towards his wrist.

*

They got to him in time and saved him. There would, of course, be no admission that such damage could have been delivered by a seventy-five-year-old girl in her slippers. The pair left town with their trinkets intact, there would be nothing more to say about it. And without the terrible hand of their bossman to herd and to drive them, the other jacks scurried back to their big city warrens.

*

'That medal? It meant somethin' big for you to do that? From the Rooshian king an' all?'

'My grandfather's All-Ireland medal. 1903. Off-the-scale thieving in my book. Up there with murdering. And never mess with a Kerry saw-lady. Certainly not if you're some jackeen.'

'But he was Rooshian? You are...'

Oona laughed. 'In his arse. He was pure Kerry—all of us. Timmy Sugrue. Sugrues. How else was I to get on in this business? Those jack lads wouldn't carry the balls to come back at a Sugrue though.'

Blackbird sat stunned in the passenger seat, his hair pulled back and his features a wan mask. Tails of fright in his eyes. Beads of sweat on his brow and on his white lips. He talked nervously. 'Whoah. You and the cuttin'.'

Oona gave a weird chuckle. 'I learn on the job. Private parties only.'

A pair of foam dice swung between them, suspended from the rear-view mirror.

Blackbird sighed. 'So much for body parts. I'm givin' up on that for an act.'

'Hopefully we'll get those broken wings up on the wire,' Oona tried some encouragement. 'And you're not taking flight. D'you hear me?' she added.

There was some colour beginning to gather in his handsome Irish face and she knew he'd no anchors, or anything left that could hold him back now.

'We'll have to get you another name. An Italian one I'm thinking Merlo. That will give you better notions... and some bit of a family to be historical about. A name, kiddo. Somewhere you're from. To get some respect. And a chance in this circus.' She laughed and suddenly grabbed the dice in her hand.

'Jesus.' Blackbird flinched. 'And a saw-lady for back-up.'

'We'll both leave that old saw carry-on behind us

now. D'you hear me?' Oona closed it off.

Blackbird picked a flyer from the dashboard and studied it a bit. Oona saw he was struggling with the names, so she helped him. 'The Electric Picnic. That's next-up for us.'

Blackbird nodded and thought of wires and saws. Sure, what else was there really? Then they settled in for the road.

MIRROR

The journalist Brendan MacGearailt didn't know how Rita Sweeney was going to react. What do you expect from someone when you are picking through their wreckage, and for the first time since you were part of that wreckage. Truth is, after all that'd gone on, it didn't bother MacGearailt that much. He'd come into the old front bar attached to Sweeney's Hotel mid-morning. There was no one about other than a couple of workmen sweeping up broken glass and fixing smashed shelves. Rita herself was nowhere to be seen. The smell of burning hung in the air, but most of the smoke had cleared. Only the finest of particles remained to filter the late autumn sun that lit ghost flames on the splintered counter. MacGearailt righted a stool on which to park his big bedraggled frame. The huge mirror on the wall behind the bar was cracked and askew, but the blistered gold lettering still spelled out a taste of whiskey for him. That man reflected there didn't look out of place in all this shit, he thought. Long after he should've hung up the boots, he was still after the stories, the chance to bang out a few more lines. And here was a story.

He figured he needn't announce himself. Rita would be expecting him. Both of them would wait, amid the devastation, trying to set the other up for the first words. A strained female voice calling from beyond an inner door got no reply, and seemed to leave it at that. MacGearailt opened his book and put on his spectacles. He'd time to read the last few sentences of Frederick Douglass's story before the voice came again, nearer, rising to almost a shout, until she copped him. Rita Sweeney stopped in her tracks and choked back her words, before recovering with a new line.

'Must be another bad breeze blowing beyond that door. What's left of it. To what do I... Come for your story?'

MacGearailt closed the book and removed his glasses. The sweeping and clattering had stopped and the static of a radio came out of somewhere. Familiar country sounds. He thought he knew all the looks of this woman. What you saw and how she saw. But now she seemed scrunched-up in a way that was new. She'll be struggling with some concealment now he thought. He tried to count the years back to when she'd been the only one from town walking with the travellers behind the hearses; the glower in her eyes and her black curly spirit causing most to look downwards. On her own again now, but how, he wondered for the umpteenth time, in the name of Jaysus had she ever ended up with Sweeney. The late Pat Sweeney. That had taken him on the blindside. Rita Mangan, the champion of the downtrodden and barrelling Pat Sweeney. Her hair now greying and brittle, but the eyes had dimmed hardly at all. A glance told him all that. It might be the mode of the widow he thought. What caught him harder though was the reflection in the smoky mirror: the sight of himself and Rita Mangan framed together again — a jolt through his hardened veins. He tried a quick thin smile, as if it could alter something, but he knew the course and he tried not to let it bother him unduly.

'Rita, the years, the years, haven't they...' It was the best he could get after he turned back to face her. The woman he thought he might have loved. Might have loved him. Once upon a time.

Her eyes strained and narrowed. She unfolded her arms and then wrapped the black cardigan tighter to her, as though that might be all the protection she had. She could have been about to say something more, when the crunching sound from around the corner of the bar caused her to hesitate. He knew Corrigan would have sensed the moment now. JC. James Corrigan, chairman of the local council, had come in by the back lane. In he came with his sly voice. He was a short, heavy man and everything about the way he was dressed seemed to want to drag him further to the floor. An enormous camel coat flung wide, an expensive blue suit — the jacket hanging almost to his knees — a massive green tongue of a tie and a weight of

polish on his brown shoes. Seemingly the only thing holding him up were the red braces that reached under his ex-
tensive belly to grip the trousers. His thin, dyed hair was
combed across a wide brow that topped a face of broken
veins, with eyes that looked like they wanted to escape.
The whole bustle of him gave off an impression of ani-
mated surprise.

'Rita.' He nodded to her and she responded by turning away and disappearing again, while Corrigan continued. 'Brendan, you're away from home ground. To
what...' Of course, Corrigan would be running the show.
'It was always a pleasure' MacGearailt interrupted,
'if that's where this has got to go.' The first cuts were in.
'But let's assume it doesn't. I'm here for...' MacGearailt
looked about him. The whiff of Corrigan's cheap after-
shave told him to stop.
'Your story. We might be forgiven for thinking that.'
Corrigan shrugged and turned away to survey the damage.

Despite all the commotion around James Corrigan,
MacGearailt had always done well to remember that behind
the standard bluster, there was a deviousness that might
pass for some intelligence. Corrigan could look stupid, but
control was what mattered, no matter how thick you might
be. To win a game was all that mattered. MacGearailt, the
journalist, understood how it went. You make your point
well. Eloquently even. And then you probably lose on
that score anyway. Arrangements of words were not what

counted most — if they counted at all. A spat-out cliché, even a single word, or indeed silence, more often than not the winner. What had the bould JC played for this time? And Rita Sweeney, what had she just lost?

There was nothing more MacGearailt needed to say for now. He'd replaced his glasses, shifted himself and picked up a framed photograph, its glass shattered. The walls around the bar had been covered in photographs of the local club teams, Fenians. Young men in stripey black and white jerseys, even from the seventies when the colour came in to reveal the same black and white, but with the added grass-stains and tints of wind-burnt complexions. And the hairstyles. Now all in this melee, some frames still hanging, some half-hanging, but most strewn among all the other breakages on the floor. MacGearailt had made his pick and was fixed on just one photograph. Last year's team. In it there were the usual fifteen, plus subs and Rita in her physio's tracksuit — a happy year as they had the cup. There was something else though. In the back row, at the edge, there was a young kid with a black face.

'The Great Black Hope. Is that what all this is about?' MacGearailt mused, in his American sportswriter's gruff, knowing the irony might not land, as he ran a reel in his mind of the athlete and his skills. As he did, he could see, reflected in the glass, Rita Sweeney appear again and then sharply turn and retreat.

'Two great feet,' Corrigan volunteered. He'd heard, and looked like he was gearing up around the real matter-at-hand.

MacGearailt ran his eye quickly over what he could see of the other photographs. Imagining this year's one —

there'd be no cup and no black face. He knew that much anyway. Corrigan would have no medals to give out. Mac-Gearailt turned back again, head down, his hands deep in his anorak pockets, like he was rooting for something, distractedly, until he reached up, removed his glasses again and placed them in a case he'd lifted from the counter. At the same time, he looked directly at Corrigan for the first time and opened his mouth as if to punctuate a question. The distracted M.O. of the journalist.

Corrigan, the politician, stayed with his own carry-on, his own distracting, by turning his back, going in behind the counter and pulling at a drawer under the cash-till. He began foostering around for something in there. MacGearailt watched him in the mirror as he closed the drawer, slipped a phone from an inside pocket of his coat, looked at it as if to reassure himself and then, not appearing to be wholly satisfied, slid the phone back into his pocket. He turned again with a grunt and settled, a confused look about him. MacGearailt had allowed himself a smile. His own phone pinged a notification. He went to his pocket and produced the phone and his glasses again. He read the message, gaped back at Corrigan, and laid the phone face down on the counter with the glasses. A look of concern came slowly over Corrigan, lingered briefly, till he got it under control. As far as MacGearailt was concerned, things were moving along nicely. Corrigan continued to busy himself like he owned the place, brushing a spot clean with a towel and plugging in a kettle, all the while checking his phone. He turned and put his hands on the counter and spoke calmly.

'I think I know where you'd like this to be going,

Brendan, but there's nothing in it you know. You'll take tea?'

'Oh I don't know. I don't really know what I'll take. You'd look good in an apron. Tea. Yes, thank you.' Mac-Gearailt was sensing the effort of the eyes trying to keep up with his own as he gazed along the broken shelves. He was also making an effort of his own... not to allow... it was ten years now. Ten years dry. The mirror showed him his own grey hair, still to his shoulders like those teams from the seventies in the photographs.

'No. That thing you wrote for the Trib back then. It was wrong. And no, there was no big row between any of us. Pat Sweeney wasn't a man for any of that kind of an argument with me. No. And neither was I with him.' Corrigan was loud in his dismissal but somehow made it sound like he was almost pleading too.

'Ah, the travellers. That ol' yoke. Well, in fairness, there was never a thirsty one as long as Pat Sweeney's was open. Poor ol' Pat. Went quick in the end. Rita seems to be making a go of it in fairness. Until all this anyway. Hard to keep up with the likes of you around though. But you always had your own cust... clients to think about. You still do.' MacGearailt teased it along a bit. 'And now your own new hotel. Sure after last night you'll be thinking about expanding? Have a lot more clients.'

'I never did a wrong thing to any traveller. I'd nothing to do with that... that thing. And I've nothing more to say about it. No. And sure you've had your say too. The reports. The articles.' Corrigan was determined not to be drawn on the present situation, keep it to the past.

MacGearailt gave the impression that he was barely

listening—that being his way with such conversations, which mostly took the course he wanted anyway.
'Amazing the number of people who don't read and are
such fucking experts on what I wrote. Or should I say
what was told to me? It's a whole new ball game with this
here, now, though.'

'No. God rest the... that evening up at the halting
site. Fire is a ferocious thing. Wicked luck.' Corrigan was
still avoiding the new ball game but MacGearailt was
happy to let it play on a bit.

'You're not still talking about the horses kicking over
a fire! There was petrol. And rags.'

'No, I...'

'You know I get so pissed off with that word. No.
Start a sentence with it and what matter how the facts are
running, you'll always get to denial. Always no. You get
to an incantation if you say it enough. The sacrament of
denial.'

'I'm not...'

'Look. Yeah. The absolute crap of all that then.
With the travellers. But what about this here? Now?'

'This town has suffered a great deal since...'
Corrigan continued to play for distraction.

'Since I wrote those things about it?'

'No. Well yes, that too. But the lives... the children.
They say the stench of burning flesh is still up around
there. Kids around here are afraid of the ghosts.'

'And so they should be. And of their own fathers
too, some of them. But then they'll still hold on to their
privileges. So long as difference isn't tolerated. No fear
of that.' That was a speech he'd heard first from Rita

Mangan before any Pat Sweeney or any fires and, as he said the words, he felt them roll into a mist before him.

Rita's re-appearance halted the roll. MacGearailt noticed the lines in her face. She was back again from whatever domain she skulked in beyond. Her eyes were set on MacGearailt, but it didn't look like she'd speak. It brought down a quietness on Corrigan too, without him even looking at her. Hanging on. Just waiting. Both of them, MacGearailt thought. Or maybe he simply hoped. He'd try to play her into the talking. He fingered his glasses and started speaking quietly, his head lowered, to draw her in.

'Rita, I'm not from town as you know. But up the road where I do come from has its own terrible past. We were all on different sides in history and God knows none of our people acquitted themselves all that well. We all come from some colour of a shirt. But it's not that now. We were fighting each other then. For the country. You could almost say we were on the same side, strange as it might sound. But now it's different. It goes to the heart of what we've become. What we accept. And it's how we acquit ourselves now that matters. But you know all that.' Now he was looking straight at her. And then at Corrigan. Everything he'd just said was for Corrigan's attention. He hesitated and began again. 'Could we not just go to the truth? If I were writing the stuff about the fire up at the travellers again, I'd be a lot harder. Call some of this man's votes the 'Golden Dawn' or something. I would. This is more of the same shit here. And now it's about the colour of skins. Not tribes. Not shirts.'

He stood up and lifted the book, held their eyes for a moment and then placed it carefully back on the counter. Then he removed his glasses again and packed them away in their case and placed it in a pocket of his coat.

Corrigan turned away again and MacGearailt saw that he didn't look in the mirror. He was avoiding it, looking around to find something to light on. And sure that was the wreckage of the bar. Of course he'd have his eye on the place now, thought MacGearailt.

'Truth.' Rita was looking at the team photograph with the black boy. She'd found her voice now. 'Truth is he had to be got... had to leave when they threatened to burn the centre. The hostel. The provision... the direct provision centre. You never wrote about that.'

Corrigan turned sharply on her while looking over his shoulder to see what way MacGearailt was going to go. He tried to haul it in.

'That's not what we...'

'Let Rita go on, JC. She's wanting to say. Go on, Rita. I never wrote about it and so? Maybe I never knew about any threat.' MacGearailt was reeling his memories again but knew how not to show it.

'Oh, I thought...' Rita pretended to be confused.

'You were saying about him having to leave.'

'Yes, I thought...'

'No, we were just talking about the accident up at the halting site. That terrible...' Corrigan tried to rescue it again.

Accident. Rita Sweeney and MacGearailt had the same sardonic emphasis in their simultaneous expression.

After the quickfire of the exchanges, no one wanted

to make a mistake. Corrigan needed to change the sub-
ject. MacGearailt needed to develop the angle that had
opened. The story. Rita needed to say her piece and get
back through her door. MacGearailt didn't need to move.
Rita couldn't move. Corrigan turned around not knowing
who to face. He turned to Rita. He found a calm voice.

'Rita. Maybe you could see if you have a drop of milk
inside.'

Rita didn't move. As he sat down again on the stool,
MacGearailt remembered the nervous mouth on her just
before she'd told him that everything was over between
them. How hard it seemed for her to do. It was the only
time he could recall her being unsure about anything. But
she was talking then to a drunk. And all that had to be
forgotten, gotten over. And so much of his memory had
dissolved since and he'd rebuilt, with the help he'd gotten,
only what mattered. But one thing that had never been
forgotten was the look on her face when she'd had to tell
him that she was now going with a man who refused to
sell him his poison. A man who, in fairness, kept his shop
open for everyone else but had barred it to MacGearailt.
So he knew that whatever she was going to say, it would
not be easy for her. She turned to Corrigan and picked it
up, her eyes beginning to glow.

'I never associated you with the fire up at the travellers. Because I didn't want to believe you'd anything
to do with it. But I saw you talking with those men who
came a few months ago, that night the talk was the ref-
ugees hostel was to be fired. There were things I heard
said by those men. There was so much angry noise that I
couldn't even hear my own thoughts. And there you were

telling me not to be worrying, there would be nothing done. And I couldn't find my voice... Now I am the one that's bombed.'

MacGearailt felt the heat from the kindling as it caught. The smoke rising. The pair of townie hoteliers now staring speechless one at the other. He lifted a Gorta collection box and blew the dust off it, gave it a shake.

'That's a fair rattle. Ye must be on different sides?'

'What do you mean?' Corrigan had turned to him with a genuinely confused look about him.

'Sure ye must be. The fire-bombs came in here yesterday, didn't they? It was hardly the travellers.'

'That's not what I'm...'

'Hearing is it? You heard it was the travellers? Are you saying there's murder coming from both sides now? Is that it? Is that what all this... A civil war we'll say?'

'There was only one civil war. And we know which side your crowd ended on.'

'Oh, we ended it alright. And got on with things. And then faced down your blueshirts when it mattered. We've said all that. But now it's a horse of a different colour you might say.'

Rita's hands went up, palms out, her eyes closed. She spoke through her teeth.

'No traveller damaged this bar.'

'Well, that's the truth for sure. I think we know that much. But it's hardly for nothing that last night's bombing was for. Was it JC?'

Corrigan's phone rang and he made his way off out of earshot. MacGearailt took out his glasses again and looked again at the picture with the black boy and heard

Rita's low voice as she came closer. She was speaking in a fierce whisper.

'Adi. That's his name. Adi. The boy and his family are safe. I knew those men were ready to burn the hostel to the ground, so I had them here for a few nights. Hidden in the back annexe. No one knew. But then I told them to go. He's with a cousin of mine in Dublin. Every night they were here, all I thought about was the boy... those men. I couldn't bear it. Again. And then I thought someone has to stand up and I thought of the hotel here and what if... Pat would have gone for it. But I told no one about that idea. I kept it very quiet, it was only an idea. Someone must have...

He could see the burn in her eyes... asking all the questions. He had answers for her too, but he stayed that.

'I'll get some milk so,' she said as she left again.

Corrigan had come back from his call and started up again in a more conspiratorial tone.

'Fair play to the bank. They'll tide her over. Insurance won't pay, I'd say. Arson. Sure this business here, we'll never get to the bottom of it. The Guards will have their work...'

He was interrupted by MacGearailt who was holding up his phone, pointing at it and looking from it to Corrigan and back. There were long moments of silence and then some sort of resignation in Corrigan. He went straight for his pocket. He threw an envelope with a harp on the counter. His voice was chilly.

'Alright. Okay. Have a look at what's inside that and

tell me what am I to do? Whose side am I on?'

MacGearailt set his phone face down beside the envelope. He opened the envelope, unfolded a letter, looked up and spoke to Corrigan as he adjusted his glasses.

'If you hadn't...' as MacGearailt cut the sentence he was pointing at his phone and wondering was that a new type of sweat he detected on Corrigan's upper lip.

It was a copy of a letter addressed to Councillor James Corrigan. It came from a Government Minister's Office. MacGearailt nodded as he read it aloud. Put simply, it noted Councillor Corrigan's support for a plan to move the Direct Provision Centre for asylum seekers to Sweeney's Hotel. Corrigan never took his eyes off him as he read. When he was finished, MacGearailt lifted his head and removed his glasses once more. He gestured with them to Rita who'd returned with a jug. He handed her the letter and gave her a sly wink. He turned back to Corrigan.

'Fair play to you, JC. You thought you had all the angles covered. Support and take the opposition out in one move? But a bit of a coincidence the gist of it got out to some people though.'

Rita was reading the letter, her face had lost all colour.

'Well I never.' She steadied herself, a hand on the counter. 'That was only a thought I had. I'd never approached anyone. No-one knew. I know the...' She turned to Corrigan, her eyes now blazing, her voice rising. 'I'd only said it to you. We were talking about Pat, the old arguments you'd have, and what he'd do...' The whole thing suddenly dawned on her. 'What did you do...who did...? You? And look what it's after bringing here to me. Only said it to you as an idea. That Pat would've liked. Never said to another soul. You...'

'Rita. It seems you might have said it to...' Corrigan interrupted.

'Didn't. I'd say,' McGearailt finished.

'I didn't,' Rita agreed.

MacGearailt held up his phone and waved it. 'Shared it with his buddies in the Golden Dawn too, I'm told.' He nodded towards his phone. 'Riding all the horses, JC. And you're here for the prize are you not? Except there's an objection, JC. Unnecessary use of the whip we'll say? Now you know why they fired you here, Rita.'

'It's wicked out there. It's a war. What way's a man to turn?' Corrigan was panicky in his resignation.

Head back, MacGearailt sucked on an arm of his glasses and looked from one of them to the other trying to guess how the land lay now. Although *he* knew. There was little comfort, like neither of them knew where they stood now. Corrigan gathered himself.

'God as my witness, I never struck a match to a petrolled rag. Ever. I know... I know there's been questions about my support. Where I stand. Yes, I suppose you could say. And by god you did, MacGearailt. But never, ever did I want that... this, whatever that... this is, to happen. Maybe there's something could be done with the insurance. We'll sort something.'

Rita had her hands in the air looking like she was about to interrupt, but then she caught a glimpse in the mirror of MacGearailt giving a shake of his head, so she steadied herself again and retreated to a thoughtful smoulder. MacGearailt, like a satisfied judge, moved in to wrap it up.

'Good. A misunderstanding is all it is.' He gave Rita a look that said she was safe. 'Ye are both on the one side after all. We're all on the one side for once so. And luckily no one is killed this time. And it'll all be paid for. That right, JC?'

Corrigan went to say something but just nodded. MacGearailt was on his feet, bending to gather more of the broken photographs. He placed them carefully on the counter, avoiding eyes. Then he put his glasses in their case, shoved that with his phone in a pocket and dusted off his coat. He left the Douglass book on the counter. There was nothing else he wanted to carry out from this place.

'Well, that's what brought me in. That's the story so. It won't be on the credit side for the town though. But a bit of decent accommodation for some folk would sort that. What do you think, Chairman Corrigan? And if you move quick, you might put out a good team again this year.' He looked one more time towards the mirror. 'Jaysus, everything looks all twisted in there. Put it straight, will ye?'

He adjusted his eyes to the low sun outside and checked again the message he had received earlier. It was from an old pal with a tip for a horse.

A FEINT

It was Margaret Moran's funeral day. Easter and the clarion daffodils had been and gone, and now the twists of wild roses and woodbine were whispering on the hedges that lined the avenue to the church. Elizabeth West grimaced as the ragged tones of the ten o'clock peals pitched into the dewy air.

'You know, Di, that actually hurts my ears,' she said to her daughter.

Diane thought her mother was entitled to her grievance as long as she kept her voice down. The two Protestant women were on their way up in the procession to Drohid Catholic church where they were to play at the funeral mass. The Wests were accomplished performers who had played in the National Concert Hall. Teaching music, they held their own against the draughts, and other temporal ravages, out at the old manse at Grange. They always walked out together, like two mythical avian creatures; bareheaded, their identical waist-length hair in fine grey veils; wrapped in wool from chin to boot; gold-rimmed spectacles on fine, beak-like noses and with the translucent complexions of the highly-bred. It was difficult to tell which of them was the mother — until she spoke, for then the brittleness would appear, the age lines more pronounced, her skin lighter and a certain dryness around the mouth. They had been asked to stand in at the ceremony by Michael John Finnerty, carpenter and church organist, who had damaged his right hand with a chisel while fixing a few boards on a boat above at the river. It would be the first time in almost fifty years that MJ would be unable to fulfil his organ duty in the church.

It looked like most of the town was making its way up the avenue. Under the stone arch of the entrance, Finnerty, an ageless wisp of a man, crouched beside the priest. Father Paul, a tall, black priest—'here on the missions' as he liked to joke (to a blank response it can be said) — was decked out in the white and gold vestments of the Glorious Resurrection. He had come in, some months previously, in place of Canon Martin Comiskey, for whom things had taken a bad turn. The Canon was now being looked after in a home somewhere. Finnerty, the bare, skeletal five foot of him, was wearing his brown suit and he reached out with his good hand to the two women as they came up the steps.

'Ladies, you are welcome. We are all most grateful.' He tapped his bandaged hand against the priest's hip.

Father Paul had been showering welcomes on the towns-people as they filed in.

'You are welcome. You are most welcome,' the priest continued to repeat as he turned briefly to the women and beamed and then turned back to his "you are welcomes". Despite all the recent to-dos, the Catholic Church was holding its own, sort of: it was still in demand for the beginning and the end, and the odd day in between. The deceased, Margaret, had remained stalwart throughout her nearly ten decades and had earned the title of 'devout woman', something which would be held forth today.

The Wests stood aside until there was a break in the long line going in, and the mutterings of 'Father', in re-sponse to the priest's welcomes, had died down. Finnerty had also kept himself back, throwing the women the odd shy, expectant glance. The priest stretched out his arms as he advanced towards the women and then, as if remember-ing something, he clasped his hands and almost bowed.

'Ladies now. I'm sure you will want to find your way to the—'

'It's just a wee bit out of sorts. The organ. It's a bitch... sorry... to tune and some of the stops and keys are sticky. The pedals have a good action though. I did a bit of oiling yesterday.' Finnerty interrupted the priest and asserted himself with the apology. The women showed no reaction.

'Right. I'm sure Mister Finnerty won't mind showing you... yes, and we can get things underway. Oh, will we see you for some lunch after... after the graveyard? Down at the Arms? No? Ah, that's a pity.' The priest had responded to the simultaneous shaking of the fine heads. He continued a little awkwardly 'MJ here, Mister Finnerty, will eh, fix up with you. You will so, Michael John? Thanks. I'd better get on stage. Oh sorry, I forget myself. Nice to meet you ladies. I should be off now.'

'We'll just play the music, if that's okay.' Elizabeth was gracious in her response.

Finnerty had indicated with his bandaged hand that they were to go in through the small door up to the balcony and Diane West gestured back with her violin case, that he should lead the way. The women gave twin polite smiles to the retreating priest, and were on their way.

The creeping Finnerty led them into the dry, dull space of the organ loft. There were a dozen or more members of the church choir waiting and there was a shy excitement in the air. All eyes were on the Wests as they marched past on Finnerty's tail. All but one of the choir were women, mostly older, and the man, a young fellow, was a Kilkelly, the butcher's son. He was blushing to his toes, although this could not be seen in the dim light. Elizabeth recognised him as someone who had been sent to her for piano lessons: he couldn't play and she reckoned neither could he sing. The Wests nodded in an unsmiling harmony as Finnerty led them over to the organ. The choir averted their eyes and busied themselves rustling through their sheet music.

Downstairs the pews were full. There were no men hanging out at the back or dossing outside the door. The men who were there were respectful and in their places alongside the women. A small column of primary school children filed into the front couple of rows. They were marshalled by two young teachers — women from the town.

There was a great shortage of younger men and women in the town, and those who were there were barely distinguishable from the older, greyer populace: young mothers fashionable but under pressure; young men with receding hair like their fathers and flushed with stress. For that was the way of it. The hardship of keeping up. No danger of starvation or raggy poverty, no death from deprivation— for those who could stay—but there were other things to ruin, or end, young life. These were solid country people, but still there was the lure of excess. The only sound in the church was of a shuffle or the echo of a cough. This was a respectable congregation held in that light that brings no image or scent from the world outside. Inside the church, the light had a special purpose: to quieten souls.

Margaret Moran's oak coffin lay on trestles at the top of the centre aisle — a spot in which she may have happily rested for eternity. It was unadorned except for a simple brass crucifix that had been taken from her house and fixed upright on the box by MJ Finnerty.

*

Margaret had no living relatives. She had lived alone in a small house on Bridge Terrace. Hers was the last habitation on the edge of the town, on the way out to the Dublin road. The terrace itself was mostly derelict and abandoned, with only Thomas 'The Fence' Garvey occupying a street-level room at the other end from

Margaret's. He lived behind a broken door and missing window panes. The Fence would spend a week putting up, or mending, stakes and wire for farmers — he ran the tightest, straightest wire imaginable; the next week he'd spend in Comiskey's public bar and the next lying on his cot recovering his body and letting his mind mend slowly. Then the whole cycle would be repeated. The whole of his life was arranged in slices of thirds: Hayes, the secondary school teacher had jokingly offered to print it all out as a pie chart for him so that it'd be in his hand, like a certificate, when he needed to explain. He'd interrupted this divvy-up for the first time since his mother died when he heard that Margaret Moran was no more: he went straight to Comiskey's for a second consecutive run at it. He wouldn't be coming to any church, or any graveyard either. The Fence'd see her off in his own fashion.

Margaret Moran was one of those souls of the earth whose time was passed in fastidious solitude. Her life didn't seem to add up to very much. There were her hens and cats. There were plain biscuits. There was a reluctance towards the ordinary rumblings of the world, almost a dowdiness. She kept to herself largely. No excitements. No loves. But she was noted. Grief had boarded with her since she lost her mother. Some part of her mind was torn. If there was one thing that enthralled her, it was the church. She would spend whole days praying and dawdling there. Helping out with the flowers and the cleaning, she was too reserved to be involved as a lay minister or with the collections. Her contribution was her steadfast, silent and reliable presence. And that was noticed. It was noticed by those who weren't running around chasing their tails. She loved to hear the choir, and loved it even more when MJ played the organ. When they were both much younger, she would sit there and listen to him practice, giggling when he went on one of his solo runs, maybe jazzing it up a bit. MJ noticed her. He thought she was a fine-looking girl and he'd liked to imagine that he was playing specially for her. Time might have seen his soft spot for her grow into something else. He was very busy though, learning his carpentry and his cabinet making; too busy in himself to recognise much about himself, to discover other passions. So apart from his work and the organ, he had no desires. As they grew older, Margaret and himself continued to share a peculiar space, all of their own. They sometimes even shared their thoughts, awkwardly.

She might say, 'Ooh, I never heard... Ooh, it was just wonderful. What you played there. I dunno it took me... I dunno, it was beautiful. No I never... '

And he might say, 'That was Bach, Margaret. That's B. A. C. H. He was a German, you know. Oh, you can't beat the Germans. I mean of course for the music. The church music anyway. I need to get more even with the bass of it. Sure maybe I'll have to fix up the old machine a bit. Oh sure look, the workman always blames his tools. Now.'

That's what he called it — the old machine. That would be it. And they would go on their ways. In later years, it crossed his mind that maybe he and Margaret, in his words to himself (and for sure to the bold Fence as well), 'might be good at something together.' He never gave a whole lot of thought to what it might be that they'd be good at though. The Fence asked him once (though the Fence had no idea after, that he did in fact ask).

'What... my friend... do you say, do you say, do you *think*... you'd be *at* together? What do you *think*... do you *say*? Huh?'

No one ever heard what Margaret would have made of all that. And if Finnerty never asked her, sure, how would anyone know? Sure, who would she say it to anyway?

*

The organ gave a false start, the pipes moaning as Elizabeth West tested a scale. The silence that followed was broken only by her own impatient muttering. Finnerty jerked on his stool. Then a note flew off Diane's violin. More silence. Then another lower, more plaintive note, and richer in tone. Finnerty held his breath. The organ replied in tune, followed by an audible sigh of relief from the older woman, and a quieter release of air from Finnerty. There was the sound of pages turning, a short choppy intro from the organ, and the choir launched into a shy 'Nearer my God to Thee'. The priest paraded onto the altar followed by his servers—a middle-aged man and woman in their civvies. Father Paul commanded his altar in a princely way as he moved briskly through the mass. Vestiges of his smile swam about him even though he had his serious face on. Like a good actor, he had 'presence'.

Finnerty had settled himself down in the shadows near the organ. He followed Elizabeth West's moves intently.

She was winning in her struggle with the creaky mechanisms, and the 'old machine' was holding up. She was able to anticipate the dud or lazy keys and stops as she pushed the choir. The choir had perked up and worked their way through a passable version of Schubert's 'Ave Maria' before they came to a satisfied rest. All the while, Finnerty watched and listened. His small, focused expression betrayed none of the tension that he was feeling. Then after a short delay, to allow everyone to settle, the priest stepped up to the microphone.

'So my good people, we remember Margaret. She was a good woman. She was true to Jesus's instruction "Love thy neighbour as thyself". Margaret was a comfort to the poor, and she was poor herself. But her spirit was not poor. No, it was rich with love. Love for Jesus. Love for His Church. Simple, simple love. Margaret was a devout woman of love.'

Father Paul went on to recount the simplicity of Margaret's life. How she was a woman of small needs and few words; how she loved her cats and her garden; how she was loved by everyone who knew her. There was a round of warm applause. He finished with a blessing, and rose on the altar to end the mass. Finnerty hadn't paid too much attention to the priest's words due to the tension rising in himself. Now he was on his feet and calling out.

'Eh. Eh, Father. Father.' Finnerty held up his bandaged right hand in an alert.

The priest stopped what he was about to do and looked up at the balcony. The congregation slowly turned to see what might be happening. The priest then remembered and went back to the microphone, tapped to check

it was still live, and said, 'Yes. Yes, of course.' The congregation turned back to the altar, and Finnerty sat
back down. The priest clasped his hands and continued.

'And now we have come to a special moment. A...
special, yes. A performance for Margaret from... yes.' He
looked to the balcony again, pleadingly. But he needn't
have worried. Finnerty had signalled to the Wests, and
the music started.

It was 'Ave Maria' again, this time by Bach and
Gounod. For violin and organ. Performed by the Wests,
mother and daughter.

Diane West started the piece on violin. The first
notes opened the door Finnerty had hoped for. The church
acoustics resonated to the playing way better than to anything that was ever played there before; as he had imagined it might, but could never really allow himself to
believe. His tension eased into a slow rapture as the piece
developed. When the organ came in, it sounded wonder-
fully different to anything he had ever achieved with his
darling machine. Elizabeth West had found her way into
the confidence of the old thing. She found the strains and
the fluency to lay down a marvellous bedrock, allowing
her daughter's violin to state clearly, and rhythmically,
the plaintive tone of the piece. The intense excitement of
his feelings was something new for Finnerty, but this path
to his enjoyment was only truly opening for the first time,
so he couldn't begin to explain it. He hoped that Margaret
was enjoying it too.

The congregation below sat in silence. A silence that
had set out reluctant had become stubborn, but was now
not wanting to end. This music went into the people's

souls, more than the light, more than any words, more
than any God could do.

Finnerty was ecstatic in himself. He felt happier
than he had ever been before. Everything he'd done had
been justified.

The music ended, the mass ended, the silence ended.
Margaret was removed to her grave and everyone carried some joy away with them. The two Protestant ladies
brought home two hundred euros. It was supposed to be
one hundred, but Finnerty was still transported when he
counted it out for them. They thanked him politely and
made off. As they walked down the avenue, Elizabeth said,
'You know Di, I believe we should have the parlour bright-
ened up. It's beginning to hurt my eyes.'

*

Later, in the evening, a very contented Michael John
Finnerty sat up beside Tomasheen 'The Fence' Garvey at
Comiskey's counter. The last of the sun washed warmly
across their workmen's hands.

'You wouldn't believe it, Fence, what I had to go
through to make sure that woman got the send-off she
deserved. I wished she could have been there to hear it.'

The Fence, on the misty verges, threw his bit in.

'But she was, MJ. I know she was. Sure wasn't I just
talkin' to her. And she saying to me "ooh it was just

wonderful... ooh wasn't it just beautiful". And I asked her who was doing the playin'? Was it MJ Finnerty on his old machine? says I. And she says "Oh noo. It was far better than that fella. Ooh, it was out of this world."'

The Fence roared out a laugh. MJ was nimble on his feet too.

'No denying it, Fence, you must've been on guard duty down at the river today, so. Like that fierce dog... what did he go by? Three heads just like you. What did they call him? Like the old salt. Where's Hayes when you need him?'

Both men laughed.

Then Finnerty flexed his right hand, gave it a shake and reached over with it to put a firm grip on his pint.

'Jesus lord,' he said, 'that feckin' bandage had me crippled all day. Anyway, I think I deserve an Oscar for that performance. Here's to all our betters!'

'You never fooled me with your ol' chisel story, MJ. Either way you didn't miss a stroke, in fairness. Never would my friend. She had the right coins on her to boot. Sure why wouldn't she, and you the feckin' ferryman an' all? What was that boat lad's name? What was that he went by? Where the feck is the feckin' schoolteacher when you need him?' The Fence gave another loud laugh, although it was never easy to work out any of the sounds he'd be making.

The night drifted on, both men sticking together while going their separate ways. Keeping each other company. Waiting for the bell.

BIRTHDAY BOYS

The two dogs stop their yapping and look over at me from the shed across the yard. Baleful. They won't come across in this rain. Are they wondering how I'll open this door? No latch, just a bit of rope. Typical. Hit it with the shoulder anyway. Gust blows me in. Feckin' rain follows me in too. Shut it out with a slam of the arse. Throw on a light. No sign of the quare lad, or that other hobo. Table in disarray, embers smouldering, kettle as black as McAdam's tar. Soot webs for decoration on the mantel. Two black cats on a dirty old mat... only see their yellow eyes. The old farmhouse has three rooms. This middle room is where everything happens. Has done for, one, two hundred years. See the crib is in place, on top of the old food safe. Normal so.

Shake out the hair.

'I'd say you didn't trim it since.'

'You fecker... I didn't see you.'

'Happy Christmas so, little brother.'

'Ah yeh, the same to yourself. Jeez Nog, what's that you have?'

I've called him Nog since I was a child and couldn't get my tongue around his full christian. Saved him from an eternal Nollaig. He has come from the dark cave that is his bedroom, holding some class of a coloured-paper decoration which he goes to pin up over the hearth.

'Ah for feck's sake, look at your own.'

'Is it dreads you have it in, or is it just more soot?'

A white gap opens in his gaunt, bristly face, and he makes the silent laugh with his great, bulgy eyes. His long dreadlocks are gathered in at the neck and slung inside a grimy collar.

'My soot locks. Hah. Did you throw your head into Little Andy's? Any sign of the other honch? On the road?'

'Nah, I walked straight up from the bus. Terrible crossing earlier. Set off the alarm at security. Is he about?'

'I haven't seen him, but I hear he's around okay. Stoppin' over at Delia's, I'm told. Last couple of nights.'

Typical JJ. He's the middle brother. Have to smile.

'He'll have had the Beatle boots off so. And polished.'

'Did you notice a black one out on the long acre? I can't see her in the back field, and I was waiting for it to stop peltin'. She'd be heavy.'

'Can't say I did.'

'It's comin' in hard alright. You came up with it against you. She'd be stupid enough to turn into it too. Go on up, into it.'

'I can't say I'd any choice in the matter, and there isn't a leaf on a tree.'

'Don't be touchy. I was sayin' that she's stupid. I'll get her when it stops.'

'I'd say it's down for the evening. You still keeping them on so?'

'Ah a couple, for the, you know, grant or whatever. The payment yoke from Europe. Know the feck. Reps. Europe be the feck.'

Nog had got the bit of land after the father had shagged off. Then he had stayed on with Mama, until she went. We brought her ashes home ten years ago tomorrow, on Christmas Day.

My oldest brother is a peculiar man, like the rest of us, I suppose. He spends half his time gadding about the country; after theatre and art, the heck. The rest he stays here, and I suppose, keeps it up. The other lad wanders about in some other direction picking up a gig here and there. JJ was in bands — showbands, rock bands — so he has his circuit. Me? In a peculiar way, I'm probably the most settled. I've lived in London for, oh, over forty years now. Started life as a class of a hippy, then tried the political stuff, you know, the revolution—where did that feck off to? Sure I got pissed off with it, so I became a punk. And then Thatcher. Feck me. So, I retired and got a job in the Council and settled down to a sweet life of work, blues, ganja and healthy food, all by my lonesome. Oh, and grew the hair again. We all do now. It's something for Mama. Swore one Christmas we'd never cut it again, none of us. Mama loved that. Her three hairy crows. Feck the rest of them.

Growing up in our house, we all read our share. Mama's people were townies, teachers and the like, so she came stocked. The father read his own stuff: *The Irish Press, Reader's Digest*. Mama swore that she got him to read Turgenev. Maybe that's why he fecked off. Nog can't remember that, but then there is a lot to forget too. Every year I bring them a book each—slim, so as not to burden them in their travels. Poetry is ideal. In fairness you would hardly think of either of them that way—if you didn't know them, that is. They are both big, strong, wild-looking men. Yeh, but how shall I put it... they have their sensitive side. JJ might draw a clout now and again—well able to—but we are all of us passive men beneath. Myself, I am of a weaker construction, being short and slight, but I have been described as wiry, and that gets me by.

'You'll like that, I think. She's the Poet Laureate now. It's a good one to carry around.'

'Thanks brother. That's brillant. Here did I tell you about that feckin' Beckett play I saw up in Dublin?'

The table is cleared back a little and tea and a couple of egg sandwiches are set up. Nog is splayed on the chair with no back, having left the one with the back to me, his gesture to my weaker frame. When JJ joins us he can use the crate.

'It was that one with the pair in the dustbins. The *Endgame*. What? Jaze I'll tell you, it was brillant! Brillant altogether. And a laugh. Oh a feckin' great laugh. Did you ever come over it? You should. I was up for a week in the hostel, there in Amiens Street. A great breakfast. I went across to that art gallery. Saw that painter buck O'Donoghue's pictures on the Way of the Cross. Brillant.'

'I see you have the crib up.'

'I do. Tradition. Hah?'

'Tradition. Yeh, I suppose. We'll all go up to the graveyard tomorrow as per usual? Are you ready this year? Any news on a headstone?'

'Nah. Didn't get back to your man. Still, he has the piece of marble got. From feckin' China no less. What the feck. Hey.'

'Hey what?'

'Hey, look what the wind blew in now. Howya buck? I was just sayin' to me other buck here that the feckin' marble comes in from China now.'

'What feckin' marble?'

'For the grave above.'

'Sure, there's no one up there.'

JJ's giving it the usual rattle. He is looking good. Great man for the suit. This time a pinstripe no less. No way am I sure about the plum shirt though. Looks like something from one of his showbands. Sure, probably is. His hair down over his shoulders in a soaked black sheen. How does he keep the colour I wonder? Although, in fairness now, he could be a man for the dye. And sure Nog the same, but he's definitely not a man for the dye. Mine all gone grey and these two bucks, ten, and what, twelve years older, and all black. I look at the kettle. Yeh, it must be from me living in the city. JJ throws down an old saxophone case and goes over to the fireplace where Nog has got a blaze lit.

'Good to see the old crib out. Tradition.'

'Yeh, me and Nog were just saying about going up to

the grave tomorrow.'

'Like I was saying, there's no one up there.'

In fairness he was right. Mama's ashes haven't been taken up yet. Her own folk didn't want her back, so where else is there to put her? Sure, what the feck else would we be talking about doing on Christmas Day anyway. I look to see what Nog will say. He's holding back, looking at his poetry book, shaping to ignore the trend that is coming about. JJ is looking into the fireplace and saying it — the thing he always brings out.

'So, I'll say it again. Isn't it way past time we brought up them ol' ashes and buried, or scattered, or whatever you're supposed to do with 'em? Nog? We say this every year and there's always some ol' reason. Didn't you say last year that you'd be ready? That you'd have the headstone and some ol' prayer or a poem or something sorted for this year?'

I have to agree with JJ. He's turned now from the fire, and I can see into his big smoky eyes, and the look is determined. There'll be no dodging this bullet, I'm thinking. No, not this year. The both of us are now looking over at Nog, who looks up, after a steady little wait. There we are: the three shaggy heads all looking at each other. Three shaggy feckers, under a tin lid that keeps us dry. Then Nog looks over at the crib.

'All right. We'll do it so.'

*

Christmas morning and the yard is flooded, but the rain has stopped and the day is cold and bright. The watery light in the room is coming in over the books packed in the deep sill of the back window. Nog comes in, all business, in his Wellingtons, with the tops rolled down. Funny I think, he's like Noah, with his pairs of dogs, cows, cats... and brothers. He is in and out doing fiddly bits and pieces all morning, and we chat away between mouthfuls of breakfast.

A half dozen fried eggs had been polished off and a whiff of burning turf and grease hangs in the air by the time JJ surfaces after twelve. His suit is all crumpled. There isn't a whole lot of talk out of him. He goes straight over to the crib and looks in at it for a while. It's a simple affair, made up of a cardboard box on its side and covered in a kind of black, crinkly paper. The opening like the mouth of hell itself, with a fairy light giving off a red glow from inside. I expect to hear water dripping. Well, there was always a drip from somewhere.

'Hey, did you fix all them leaks or what?'

The crib had never changed, not since I can remember. Like the house — other than the thatch is off now. The tin up, and the new toilet tacked onto the back wall. I look into the maw of the crib. There's the baby, a baby king with his crown and his other king things; the world and the wand yoke held splayed out, his little legs crossed. A snatch of straw, kept from the old roof, makes up the little manger for the baby to lie in.

That Christmas we brought the ashes home, we divided them up in three. We'd each of us had the fill of one of Nog's Old Holborn tins. The idea, I suppose, was that we'd each of us have our own, well, piece of Mama, to keep in comfort... our own way. Whatever about anyone else's, it was always understood that the home ashes, Nog's, would be properly buried or whatever, in case anyone was ever coming back — say after we'd all be gone — you know, to pray or whatever. Visit. The other two-thirds of Mama could wander around with JJ and myself, as I said, for comfort. Nog kept dragging his heels on it, but sure something would have to give; we needed to put some of Mama to rest. Anyway, that was the sum of it.

My own tin was always sitting there, on a table or a shelf, wherever I fetched up. Well actually, I had moved them for a while to a wooden box that Sha, fuck, had given me. It came from India I think. I used to keep my dope in it... then my Mama. For a while I had a little, like holy, cloth over it and would often uncover it and light a candle and a few joss sticks and play 'My Sweet Lord'—that George Harrison song. A little ceremony. Out of it. Oh yeh, tears. Back safe in the tin now though.

Don't know what's the story with JJ's. Things have a habit of detaching themselves from that man. Like he leaves things in places. Doesn't really lose stuff, just moves on without it. And then, usually, the stuff catches up, somehow. Used to keep the tin in that old sax case. That's always somewhere he can get at it; has to be if he gets a gig. Has it with him now. Wonder if the tin's still in it? Of course he might have tried to shove them up his nose too. He'll play something if we ever get graveside. Remember him blowing that thing when he was a kid. Fourteen, fifteen whatever. I must have been five or six. Loved the sound. Blues. Mama got him those American records in Cork. The father used to say he'd be better off with the cattle in the house. Maybe that's what drove the ol' man away. Left when I was ten. One day he was just... not there. I can only remember Mama hugging me and she not crying at all. No tears, just a surge of energy in the house. Nog was around, but seemed to be out always, away in a far field. He never spoke about it then, or now. JJ was already gone with the bands.

*

It's getting late in the day, and we're waiting for Nog to come out of the toilet so's we can get the show on the road. JJ and myself have found old wellies and now we're like navvies waiting for a pick, the tops of our boots turned down, like Nog. JJ, in his suit, looks like a construction boss and is getting on to Nog again. He shouts in at him.

'Well, for feck's sake. How much can a man piss?'

'Will you hould your donkey out there. I was out of paper.'

'And what did you use. Ya dirty...'

'I've a stack of old Musical Expressos that I'm workin' through...'

'Ya feck, they're mine.'

Nog is out now, beaming.

'Will ya feck off. I've other bog rolls, just couldn't put my hands on 'em, and, when I did... let's say they were damp. But I didn't use your feckin 'old NMEs, haven't a notion where they are.'

'And you used damp bog roll?'

'Yeh.'

'Your're a feckin' animal. What are yeh?'

Nog is giddy now, laughing, and he grabs JJ into a headlock. JJ is scuffling about, banging Nog's legs with a fist, laughing even louder. They bang on into the food safe and the crib starts to rock. I grab at it and stop it falling. A shepherd tumbles out onto the stone floor and loses its head. The tiny sound of plaster snapping stills the commotion.

'Ah, for feck's sake, men.'

Nog lets JJ out, and then his big black head pushes past me. He is looking into the crib, all concerned. His massive hands reach in, gently lifting the baby and taking an Old Holborn tin from under the straw. He leaves the baby back down and carries the tin, cupped in his hands, slowly to the table. His eyes, all soft, are on the tin as he brings it into the last of the sunbeams from the back window. Rust marks streak the orange and white cover and the brassy box of the tin. He sets it down gently. It looks at home there on the faded pattern of the creamy oilcloth, among the egg stains and breadcrumbs. JJ has straightened himself and come around to look. We all lean in over the little tin. Nothing needs to be said. We've each of us perfected our silent prayer over the long years.

*

Outside, the ground is saturated but the air is crisp and the blue of the sky is paling; shortly it will deepen into sunset. We leave the yard and fall into single file for the march up the hill to the graveyard. Nog leads, JJ in the middle with his sax case and me bringing up the rear. There are only a few houses on either side in the half-mile up. It being Christmas Day, each is its own oasis of warmth and peace. This is the day when everyone is in. Even from the road you can feel the ease that has entered these simple cottages. Coloured lights sparkle: inside on trees and outside on eaves and walls and trees again. There is a glow from the TVs.

There was never a television brought into our house, but we always had the best of fare at Christmas. Mama saw to that: good food, drink when we were old enough, and reading and talk. Debate was what she lived for. Rights and wrongs. Ins and outs. So no matter that our schooling ended early (only I finished secondary), we all three had gone into the world wisened-up because of Mama. No doubt that each of us is thinking something like that as we go on up.

'They'll all be lookin' at the three of us now. Pass no heed.'

Nog is not meaning to be unfriendly; he is just minding our attempt at being, well, solemn. Yeh. I imagine there are signals of goodwill towards us from most of the families as we pass. Jim Sullivan is shaking his stick, like an irate priest, but it turns out he is only pointing out the black cow that has settled in his road field. Nog acknowledges this and we keep on.

'We'll take her with us on the way down. She's very

close to droppin'it. We'll have another birthday.'

The graveyard is down a short lane between two fields. It is set out beside the ruin of an old church, on a slope that looks into the valley. The hill behind affords some protection from the worst weather. This would have been the original settlement in these parts. Down below is a sort of scribbled landscape of wet fields, stone walls and briary ditches, with a rise up the far side to the south, and sure eventually, if you keep going for thirty miles, there'd be the sea. We walk in through wild grasses studded with grey headstones. Over near a low wall of hairy stones there's a patch that looks like it has seen a scythe or a billhook.

'I came up last week and cleaned it up a tad. There should be an old spade there in along the wall.'

Making myself useful, I go over and find it, a cold damp inanimate thing. I look to Nog and he is gesturing toward two rocks that form a crevice.

'If we make a bit of a hole there it should do the trick. What do ye think?'

JJ shrugs his frame.

'That looks like the job.'

I start to root out some weeds and chop into a few sods to create a place. When I start digging brown soil, I get a weird feeling that I am disturbing something different. It's the way the clay is crumbly and dry, despite all the rain.

'She's a well-drained site here. That's the way they picked 'em.'

Nog takes out the tin and is wrapping it in a plastic bag he has brought. JJ is unpacking his sax case and taking out a little tin too. Feck. He hands it to Nog.

'Here put these in too. I'm not great anymore for the comfort and... well you know...'

I stop digging and lean the spade against the stone wall. I reach into my coat pocket and draw out my own little tin. I offer it to Nog.

'Like I said, set the alarm off at security... better...'

Now we are operating in silence again as Nog is wrapping the three tins together. His head is down but I can tell he is in difficulty. We all are. I carry on and finish the spadework while JJ clips the sax around his neck. This is it so. The hole is a foot down and neat in against the rocks. Nog looks at us as much to say who's going to do this. JJ and I gesture to him to get on with it. He kneels down and carefully places the package into the ground. He takes clay between his fingers, sprinkles it down and then stands up with a sigh, or a sob. We copy the business with the clay, and then we all stand tight together, heads bowed, and quiet. Once again, nothing needs to be said. Like I said, we've each of us our own prayer.

The evening sun is now sitting down beyond the hill. JJ's sax is a tin-opener on the silence. He is playing the opening bars of the dance-tune 'The Hucklebuck'. Mama's favourite. Maybe that's why the father fucked off. The notes swell and fly out from the hillside. Back in the stillness, we shuffle into our own private places. Like three ancient birds, we perch for an age, our feathers tucked in, and each possessed of a withered stare.

On the way down, we carefully drive the black cow and see her into the outhouse with the straw bed. We have a meal of corned beef and potatoes and open a bottle of whiskey. I bring out a tube of wasabi paste which I have brought over. JJ grabs it and throws it over to Nog when I try to get it back. They toss it between them, with me as pig in the middle, and it is a bit of gas until Nog tosses it in the fire. That stops the play. There is a long silence in which I try not to sulk. Nog finds a way to apologise. After that the talk is light, like I suppose we've almost done enough being brothers... sons... for one day. Maybe we are relieved and can start to let our years catch up. JJ glues the head back on the shepherd, and spends a while staring into the crib. I sit on the crate over by the fire, and start to doze. Nog is at the table with his book. JJ is first to speak.

'So that's that so. I don't think I'll come next year. It's done. Put me on the headstone.'

'Me too. It's a fair old trek from over the water. And as you say, it's done.'

Nog closes over his book and he looks from one of us to the other.

'Did you pair talk about bringin' your, you know, tins, together so?'

JJ and myself had not. JJ is looking over at me.

'Well?'

'I've brought mine over with me every year.'

'Me too. Mama — the tin — has always been in my sax case.'

Nog is open-mouthed. 'Well what the... feckin' brillant... what was all that about?'

Indeed, no one had ever said. I'd no idea JJ had done that. All minds working, but not together. Nog is up between us and looking agitated.

JJ again. 'As far as I was concerned, it was your

move. You had the home ashes somewhere. Not that either of us had any idea where you had them... 'til today that is. It was always up to you to make the move. I was happy enough to wait. I was always bringing Mama home.'

'Same as that.' I added, 'Sure we all knew they'd have to go together, sometime, when we were ready. When you were ready.'

'Well ye pair of feckers and I was holdin' out, I dunno, until today when... ah feck it, I thought ye'd both lost yours, used them, whatever the feck. I wasn't about to give mine up, but they were startin to freak me out.'

And so it went back and forward, and back again; sure we were getting it all off our chests, until the cow called us out to welcome the new boy.

ACKNOWLEDGEMENTS

Acknowledgement is due to the following publications in which versions of some of these stories first appeared: *Surge: A Collection of New Irish Fiction* (O'Brien Press); *The Manchester Review*; *The Lonely Crowd*; and *The Art of Lying* (TCD). 'Dressed for the Kill' won the Maria Edgeworth Prize for Fiction in 2022.

My eternal gratitude to all those who, over the years, have encouraged me to read and write.

I particularly want to thank Maur for the endless spirit of her encouragement, support and companionship, which springs, of course, from her own marvellous dedication to literature.

Were it not for the faith and enthusiasm of Lisa Frank and John Walsh I wouldn't be writing these words here today. Thanks folks!

My special and eternal gratitude to Helen Meany for her wisdom and invaluable attention and to John O'Donnell for all his assistance.

Thanks to Cormac Kinsella for his commitment and expertise.

There are good and able friends who offer wise counsel to any literary aspirant and mine are John McAuliffe, Martina Evans, Richard Ford, Cian Ferriter and Catriona Crowe. My thanks to all of you.

Special thanks too to Christine Dwyer Hickey and Joe O'Connor for reading this work.

My gratitude to Ian McGuire, John Lavin and Martin Doyle for publishing early stories.

Thanks also to other friends who have read some stories, helped or egged me on over the years including Paula Meehan, Anne Haverty, Colm Tóibín, Mark O'Rowe, Liz Nugent, Theo Dorgan, Mary O'Malley, Niall MacMonagle, Paul Fahy, Liz Kelly, Tomás Hardiman, Liam Parkinson, Eithne Verling, Kevin Williams, Bren Kennelly, Doireann Ní Bhriain, Marian Richardson, Vivienne Shields, Charles Crockatt, Jim Shapiro, Mary Creggan, Nuala Hayes, Ron Carey, Andy Pollak, Paul Lenehan, Bill Barich, Anna Farrell, Shay Murphy, Eoin Loughlin, Shem Caulfield, Michael Good, Fionnuala Gilsenan, Brian Kiely, Damian Downes, Frank Macken, Éamon Little, Mary Kennelly and my great chum and fondly remembered (and erstwhile collaborator-in-theatre) Art Ó Briain. I'm very grateful to an old pal Tony Cafferky for some very early and telling illumination from his literary searchlight.

Thanks too to all those in the Oscar Wilde School in TCD; Gerry Dawe, Deirdre Madden, Chris Binchy, Declan Hughes, Jonathan Williams and all those fellow students I spent many happy hours telling fibs with — may they all continue to see truth and prosper.

Thank you to all those associated with the Maria Edgeworth prize, particularly June Caldwell, for honouring me in 2022.

I'm lucky to have a family of my own that I love dearly — so thanks to my wonderful daughters Ailbhe and Bébhinn and their partners David and Natalie, my grandchildren Lorcán, Órán and Ruán, my outrageously talented and faithful sister Finola and her family, Anna and Philip.